IROTH

TAMSIN LEY

TWIN LEAF PRESS

Keeping his Iki'i shielded so any nearby Kirenai couldn't identify him, Iroth adjusted the formal human clothing covering his matrix and took a moment to gather his senses. Using the teleport always left him woozy, and the transportation web around Earth had obviously been set up in a hurry, without the usual buffers to mitigate discomfort.

He inhaled slowly. The warm night air was full of the sound of chirping insects. Beneath his feet, fine blades of vegetation had been shorn to an even length, though he couldn't discern the color in the feeble light coming from the poles several paces away. A few other Kirenai in the shape of blue humans were already moving along a concrete path toward the sounds of a gathering crowd.

He straightened his shoulders and stepped onto the trail. Tonight, he was on an exclusive guest list full of high-ranking dignitaries and wealthy merchants. The teal-blue human shape he now wore was similar to the one he grew up using—his mother was Fogarian—though his current form was taller, less hairy, and lacked claws and fangs. But it wasn't the shape that made him uncomfortable, it was the role he needed to play.

Normally, he preferred to do his jobs as a servant or underling, blending in with the natives. He was a *burendo*, able to change both color and shape, though for this job he was to be obviously Kirenai. He charged his clients exorbitant prices, making a very comfortable living infiltrating events to gather diplomatic intel or smuggling contraband. Tonight he was after different cargo. *Live* cargo. And the only reason he'd agreed was because the purchase would be legal, for a client who didn't want the transaction made in his own name.

Striding along the path, Iroth examined a pair of females who stood shoulder-to-shoulder as they watched the guests pass by. He'd worked with the black market long enough to have heard rumors about human captives capable of inciting passion in the most reticent partners. Tonight marked the first legal event for human bondservant contracts, and competition would be high.

The females he looked at now each wore a long dark gown, one with sparkles and the other with a skirt that turned sheer at mid-thigh to reveal shapely legs. *Not bad looking*, he acknowledged, smiling at them as he passed. The one in the sparkly dress locked eyes with him, and he opened his Iki'i briefly to feel her emotions.

She was curious and a bit nervous. He understood how she felt—the first job he'd hired himself out for had been thrilling and nerve-wracking, and he'd been glad when it was over. He could hardly imagine wanting to sell himself long-term to a single person.

He continued past them, heading toward a raised platform illuminated by lights. His gut churned and his matrix wanted to contract into the smallest form possible at the sight. No matter how many times he saw a stage, he always battled those feelings. *You're not revealing yourself to anyone*, he reminded himself. He wouldn't be changing color or escorted away by his parents in shame.

No one here knows what you are.

Still, he sat at a table at the outer edge of the audience, taking some comfort in knowing he could bolt at a moment's notice. Although the emperor had forbidden ship landings on the planet and restricted access through the teleportation web, Iroth had managed to land an unmanned, cloaked ship outside the city several days ago. He'd only used the transportation web tonight in order to be documented as a bidding guest. But ever since he'd had a job go sideways and leave him stuck in the slums on a G'naxian moon for six revolutions, he made sure he always had alternate ways to get off-planet.

A human male approached his table carrying a tray with tall thin glasses of a golden beverage, and another human offered a selection of local food. Iroth politely took one of each but set them aside untouched. He'd never enjoyed foreign foods very much, plus he was too busy examining the human females gathering to one side of the stage. Each one possessed a quadruped, either on a leash or cradled like a baby. He hadn't been warned this species required accommodations for an additional life form, and made a mental note to demand additional payment when he delivered the female.

A small white quadruped put his front paws against the legs of the female holding its leash, stubby tail wagging. It reminded him of a baby *nezumi* he'd found as a child, a downy creature with a stubby tail and long floppy ears. It had been cowering in one of the space station's condenser pipes. Most residents considered the creatures pests, and the poorer families on the station hunted and ate them. But he'd put the baby into his pocket and taken it home, sneaking it crumbs of their precious food. When his father found out, he was furious. They'd eaten *nezumi* soup that very night.

Iroth shook off the memory and refocused on the human females. Now was not the time to fall into dark thoughts.

A black-haired beauty in a sleeveless burgundy dress caught his eye. The fabric was shimmery without being gaudy, and detailed with layered pleats across the bodice and a smooth skirt that draped effortlessly from her hips. Her rich golden brown skin reminded him of well-polished *amai* wood and made him wonder if she smelled as sweet.

The quadruped on her leash had thick red-and-black fur over its back and a heavy white ruff that continued down to its front feet. The animal's mouth hung open in what looked like a smile, and though his Iki'i was closed, he imagined the complete adoration the creature must have for the female.

Bid on her, a voice inside him urged. He pictured how she'd look splayed across the silken sheets of his bed, dewy-eyed and yearning for his next touch. Except he wasn't buying a bondservant for himself. His client wanted breeding stock, and the woman in the burgundy dress deserved better. He forced his gaze away, examining the other females.

The lights went down, and the auction began with the booming voice of an auctioneer rattling off information too fast for his universal translator to process. Spotlights appeared across the stage, and the women paraded out with their pets as a group, performing some sort of rehearsed strut in time to a pulsing tune. Then they retreated to the sidelines.

Iroth folded his hands in his lap and waited as the women reappeared one-by-one, letting the first two come and go without bidding. The guests were competitive, and the bids were high. Iroth's client had provided a generous allowance for the auction and said Iroth could keep whatever he didn't spend, but at this rate, winning a female would require him to spend the full amount. *Another reason to charge extra for the pet.*

Sighing, he bid on the next woman and lost. He eventually won a small female in a pink dress named Susan, who had luscious curves and perfectly straight white teeth. She bounced down the stage steps, followed by a black quadruped with droopy ears and a long tail. The animal trotted up and stuck its head on his lap while the female set a tall green bottle and two empty glasses on the table. "Ish fremmich zeze genzuln!"

He blinked, trying to decipher her words while pushing the quadruped's muzzle out of his crotch. The damn universal translator must be on the fritz. Glancing around to be certain any nearby Kirenai were otherwise occupied, he unshuttered his Iki'i a fraction, hoping it would allow him to glean some of her meaning. She was friendly and seemed to want to begin her bondservant duties by providing him a drink.

He smiled and nodded.

She set the bottle down and pulled out the chair next to him, scooting it so close that they brushed elbows. Her animal lay on the ground under the table, hot breath fanning his shins. Now that he had secured a female, he was ready to depart, but it would draw undue attention to leave before the auction was over. So he continued to smile and nod as the female chattered incoherently.

On stage, the woman in the burgundy dress appeared, knuckles white as she gripped the leash to her quadruped in both hands. The animal seemed to sense her mood, and nudged the back of her knee, herding her forward. His estimate of the creature's value increased.

She slowly walked to the front of the stage as two Kirenai and a Khargal began a bidding war for her contract. He could barely contain himself from joining in. But what would he do with a second female? After a few volleys of bidding, the auctioneer declared a Kirenai at a table in the center the winner, and the woman descended the steps to greet the new owner of her contract. Jealousy heated Iroth's center.

The female he'd purchased nudged his arm. Turning his head to look at her, his mouth collided with something that left a paste on his lips. He drew back instinctively, realizing she held a brown disk of food topped with a pale creamy substance.

"Servi." She cringed and popped the item into her mouth, chewing. "Is good," she said around the food.

She was pulsing with anxiety, struggling hard to make him like her. He licked the residue from his lips. The flavor wasn't unpleasant, slightly sweet with a hint of oil. Her wash of relief reached him, and she smiled, raising her flute expectantly. He lifted his, and she clinked the glasses together before drinking. He sampled the bubbly alcohol, finding it acceptable, though he preferred tea.

The auction ended on an overpriced female in a blue dress, garnering a deafening roar of applause from the audience. Then a band struck up a lively tune.

"I leeb dis zong! Tancen?" Without waiting for his reply, his female grabbed his hand and pulled him toward a grassy area where two other couples were moving in time to the music.

Reminding himself this was likely the last evening the female might ever have on her home planet, he let her guide him through some rhythmic steps.

A scream shattered the music.

Iroth twisted toward the sound and saw a woman backing away from her chair in horror.

At the table next to her, a Kirenai half rose to his feet, quivered for a fraction of a second, and collapsed into his resting state. Another woman fell over backward in her chair.

Iroth stared, horrified. Kirenai didn't shift to their resting states in public. Ever.

Humans began screaming and fleeing as Kirenai at other tables also collapsed. The two Khargals grabbed their females and flew up to the stage. A Fogarian tunneled into the ground. The two Kirenai who'd been dancing next to Iroth shuddered, turning into puddles right before his eyes.

He opened his Iki'i to the fullest, looking for an explanation. *Are they dead?* His species weren't easy to kill. But he could detect no emotion, no signature coming from the Kirenai nearby. This was a massacre unlike any he'd known.

He looked for his female, intending to flee with her, and realized she was gone. He glanced back toward the tables. Only two other Kirenai remained standing besides himself. The nearest one stepped closer, and Iroth felt the sharp prod of inquiry along with a sense of ammonia against his Iki'i as the Kirenai sought his identity.

Kuzara, his Iki'i was open. He shut it down, but not before sensing a brief whiff of satisfaction from the other.

Iroth's insides quivered. *You're going to be blamed for this.* No one trusted a *burendo.*

Then, to his relief, the Kirenai shuddered and collapsed along with the others.

Feeling queasy, Iroth glanced toward the single remaining Kirenai who was now striding his direction with fury in his gaze. *You can't stick around for questioning.* He had to blend in. It was what he was good at.

Taking a deep breath, he sealed his Iki'i deep inside and let his matrix relax, joining the rest of the fallen. Only a medical scanner could now tell he was alive.

He hoped he'd get a chance to slip away unnoticed before the real investigation began.

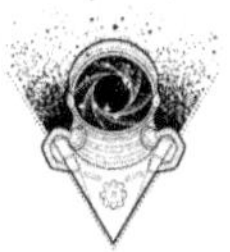

2

*M*aise pressed her back against the stage and gaped at the puddle of goo that moments ago had been her alien date. Her sheltie, Bixby, stood steadfastly at her side, warm thick fur pressed against her skirt as people screamed and ran, toppling chairs and shattering champagne flutes. Mounds of quivering alien remains dotted the grass.

She'd been the first volunteer for her friend Georgie's charity auction, glad to help the animal shelter outside of donating services from her pet grooming business. The event had brought in an exorbitant amount of money.

Except dead aliens can't pay. She felt guilty about the thought even as it flitted through her mind.

An escaped poodle sped toward her, and Maise instinctively stepped on its leash, stopping it in its tracks. The owner raced up, breathless, thanked her, and grabbed the leash before continuing her flight.

Maise returned her attention to the puddle near her feet. Was there anything she could do to help? She wasn't a doctor, but had spent the past eight years taking night classes to become a vet. Gathering her courage, she stepped closer to for a better view and grimaced. All the veterinary training in the world couldn't prepare her for how to perform triage on something that looked like a giant blue amoeba. She shuddered and backed away again. No way was she going to touch it without gloves.

"Sorry, dude. Wish I could help." She bit her lip and looked around, hoping to spot one of her friends. Everyone had already fled.

The two horned, gray aliens had jumped onto the stage behind her and now roared in what she could only assume was aggression.

She decided it was time for her to get out of here, too.

Bixby stayed in a close heel as they avoided the various splotches of blue goo scattered around the tables. There was no way any of these poor aliens were alive. She pressed a hand over her middle, wondering how many had been disintegrated.

As they passed by one of the tables, Bixby paused and emitted a low whine. The sheltie had failed service training as a medical alert dog because she was too friendly with people, but she still had a keen sense for when something was wrong with someone.

Maise stopped, wondering if she'd found a survivor. Lifting the edge of the tablecloth, she peered beneath it.

An enormous Great Dane Maise emerged, its gray fur covered in slick, dark blue goo.

She recoiled. "What have you been rolling in?"

The Great Dane froze, trembling.

"Aw, you poor scared baby." She unhooked Bixby's leash and created a noose, knowing the sheltie would stay by her side without restraint. Patting her thigh, she said, "Come here, Big Boy."

The massive dog didn't move, regarding her with turquoise eyes. He didn't look aggressive, but she knew better than to assume he wasn't. A dog his size could probably take her out with one swipe of his massive paw.

"The big ones are always the shyest, aren't they?" She spoke in a soft voice, maintaining eye contact. "Come on, Big Boy."

The dog inched forward as if pulled by a thread, stopping just out of range. His tail wagged slightly.

Bixby darted out behind him and nipped at the Dane's heels, driving him forward. Heart racing, Maise looped her spare leash around his neck and cinched it, preparing to keep the bigger dog from turning on Bixby.

The Great Dane gave the sheltie a withering glance and turned back to Maise. She gripped the flimsy leash, knowing it wouldn't stop him if he really wanted to get away. He must've slipped his collar somehow. "Stick with me, Big Boy. We're gonna find your momma."

"Ma'am, are you all right?" A voice behind her made her jump, and she turned to see a man in a dark suit approaching. A helicopter thumped past overhead.

"I'm fine." A small cluster of women moved past her, shepherded toward the stage by another man in a suit. "What's going on?"

"We're gathering survivors. Please come with me."

Survivors. Her stomach churned thinking about how many people she'd seen dissolve. "How many are dead?"

"Don't worry, ma'am, it looks like just the blue aliens were affected."

She didn't like his cavalier attitude, but didn't have a chance to respond as a labradoodle ran up to them dragging its leash. She grabbed it, adding the dog to her menagerie before joining the other women at a table that'd been pulled away from the others. The gray aliens were no longer on stage, and armed men in uniforms were extending ribbons of caution tape between stakes in the grass.

"Please hand over your cell phones," said a man with a clipboard and a bin.

"Why?" asked one of the other dates from the auction, planting her hands on her hips.

"A matter of national security, ma'am." The man held out his hand expectantly. "Please don't make us search you."

The woman harrumphed and handed over her phone. Maise reluctantly did so, too, a sense of foreboding settling over her. She'd seen enough TV shows to suspect she could end up locked in some secret government facility where no one saw the light of day. *I wish I'd called Mom and Dad one last time.*

A familiar "baroo!" split the air, and Maise turned to see a Redbone Coonhound leading a guard toward them.

"Pepper!" she called, scanning the dimness behind him for her friend Lora.

The coonhound pulled the man straight over and began nuzzling Bixby.

"This dog belong to you?" the guard asked.

Heart thundering, she said, "She's my friend's."

He shoved the end of the leash into Maise's hand. "Here. You can take her then."

"Wait, what about—" But the man was already striding away. She scowled. "Asshole."

The dogs had to sniff each other, and within moments, all four leads were tangled. Maise moved to a grassy spot nearby to give the animals more room to play. At the edge of the police tape, someone else was arguing about having her cell phone taken, and a woman in a black strapless dress sat at a table with her face in her hands.

A tall, blue, bare-chested alien approached, escorted by two suited goons. A familiar auburn-haired woman in a crimson gown limped beside him.

Pepper bayed in recognition, and relief flooded Maise at the sight of her friend. "Lora! Over here!"

Lora was a police officer, and if she had anything to say about things, nobody would be locked in a secret government facility. Her friend met her at the police tape. "Thank God you found Pepper." Lora bent to let the wriggly whining coonhound nuzzle her ear. "Can you watch her for a bit longer? I'm on duty."

"Sure." Maise had faith that her friend would soon set things right. "Whatever I can do to help."

Maise went back to the grassy area with the four dogs. Pepper and the labradoodle resumed rolling around, chewing on each other's ears. Usually, Bixby liked to be in the middle of the fray, but she snuggled up next to the Great Dane who had laid down with his massive head morosely on his front paws. Bixby kept checking in with Maise, as if expecting her to do something.

Lowering herself to sit cross-legged on the ground next to the giant dog, Maise gingerly rubbed behind his ears. His fur felt sticky and the slight odor of men's cologne hung around him—either the mess he'd rolled around in had been wearing it, or his owner was male. *What if his master was someone who'd melted?* Her chest tightened and tears pricked her eyes. "You worried about your master, Big Boy?"

He sighed, a shiver rolling across his sleek gray coat.

The other dogs wore themselves out, eventually lying down around her on the lawn. Maise grew sleepy, too, and lay back on the grass, wishing she could get out of this constricting dress. She startled awake at the sound of Lora's voice calling for attention nearby.

"We're going to speak to everyone individually about the events this evening," said Lora, addressing the gathered women. "Then we'll let you go home."

Maise headed over, and Lora reached for Pepper's leash. "Thanks for taking care of her, Maise. I'll talk to you first."

Several women grumbled about playing favorites, but Lora led her to a small table at the bottom of the stage stairs.

Maise looped the leashes of the other three dogs on the railing before joining her friend. "Do you know what happened to Georgie? I haven't seen her."

Their friend had planned the entire auction, but Maise hadn't seen her since the disaster. She hoped Georgie had been able to get away before things took a turn for the worse.

Lora rubbed the back of her neck. "She's, ah, on a space ship with an alien prince. I glimpsed her when Zhiruto Facetimed them or whatever aliens call it."

"A space ship?" Maise gasped, glancing toward the dark sky. The faintest glow of dawn lit the horizon. "Is she okay?"

"Yeah, I think so. At least, Zhiruto says she's not in danger."

Maise turned her gaze back to her friend. This was the second time Lora had mentioned that name. She thought of the shirtless alien Lora'd been walking beside earlier. "Who's Zhiruto? Your alien bodyguard?"

Lora flushed. "He's working for the prince. I'm just his NSA liaison."

Maise wiggled her eyebrows. Leading an investigation with a hot, shirtless guy was probably like a dream date for Lora. "Ooh la la."

Lora crossed her arms and scowled. "There are more than a dozen dead aliens only footsteps away. Definitely not the time to be thinking of hot guys."

"You're right." Maise dropped her gaze guiltily. "This entire thing is awful."

"Let's get on with a few questions so I can let you go home, okay?"

Maise nodded.

"Does everyone here seem normal to you? I'm looking for anyone who seems less shocked than they should be. Or more shocked. Anything strange at all."

Maise thought for a second. "I think people are acting pretty normal. Heather's been crying non-stop. Meg's her usual bossy self. I suppose Tammy's been a little quieter than usual, but I think she's in shock. I overheard someone say she and her date were kissing when it happened." She glanced to where poor Tammy sat with her knees up and a wool blanket over her shoulders. "You should probably talk to her next so she can get out of here."

"Thanks, Maise." Lora rose. "I'll let the guards know you're clear to leave."

"Thank you. Call me when you get a chance." Maise gathered the dogs and moved to the guard with the confiscated cell phones. She'd put the labradoodle and the Great Dane in the Yappy Hour kennels until she could swing by the shelter and borrow the chip scanner. Hopefully, she could get them back to their owners.

A man in a suit flashed her his NSA credentials, warned her not to speak to the press, and gave her a number to call immediately if she began to feel ill or unusual.

"You mean if I feel like I'm about to dissolve into a lump of Jell-O? Because I'm pretty certain no one had time to make a call before they dissolved."

The guard looked at her blandly. "If we thought you were in danger, we wouldn't allow you to leave."

Yet another guard escorted her to her Jeep in the parking lot and left her to load up the dogs. The back of her Jeep wouldn't hold all three animals, and she had to put the massive Great Dane into the passenger seat. It was now four in the morning, and all she wanted to do was sleep. She headed to the Yappy Hour and pulled up to the service entrance. With the enticement of a handful of kibble, the labradoodle pranced happily into a kennel. The Great Dane wasn't so easily swayed.

"Come on, Big Boy." She rattled a stainless steel dish. "Aren't you hungry?"

She could swear he shook his head no as he sat on the floor between the cages. He lay down with his head on his front paws.

Bixby nosed him, then began licking his face. Maise frowned. Bixby wasn't a licker, but it was what she'd been trained to do during her service days to alert her owner of an oncoming seizure.

What if whatever he rolled in is what's making him sick? "Oh, God. Bixby, no. Get back."

She pushed the sheltie aside. She had to get that stuff washed off before he became more seriously infected or infected anyone else.

Tugging on his leash, she got him to his feet and led him through the kennel area to the washing stations. She had the Dane hop onto the table and tied off the leash, then stepped out of her restrictive gown. There was no one else here, and Ted wouldn't be in until nine.

Dressed in nothing but a strapless bra and panties, she turned on the water.

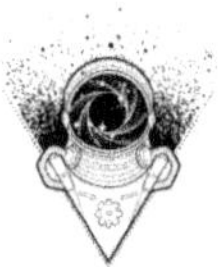

3

*T*roth's breath caught at the sight of the female's bare skin. Long, golden brown legs. A smooth flat abdomen with a perfectly dimpled navel. Pert breasts covered with brown fabric that he yearned to push aside so he could gaze at what lay beneath. *Kuzara,* how he wished he didn't have to hide behind his current shape.

The Great Dane had been an excellent choice for a disguise, despite how difficult it was to maintain a quadruped. He'd even felt a bit smug when the prince's bodyguard had looked straight at him and moved on. But as the night progressed, he'd begun feeling unwell. Keeping his matrix compressed into a smaller size was causing his exterior to leak interstitial fluid like a film of sweat, and he could no longer shield his Iki'i. His head throbbed, and he shivered with the need to resume a more familiar shape.

"It's okay, Big Boy. You'll feel better after we get you cleaned up," the woman called Maise said as she filled a bucket with soapy water.

He was glad the universal translator seemed to be working now, but despite the female's words, he felt her worry like a knife. Maise was as kind as she was beautiful. Her gentle touches behind his ears and the soothing tone of her voice made him want to curl up around the fullness of her body and enjoy her in other ways.

She poured warm water over his neck and shoulders. The soap smelled like sun-warmed citrus flowers, mingling with her feminine musk as she leaned close to scrub his coat with a red, nubby thing. Her touch along his back and over his sides felt so good. Under other circumstances, he would've enjoyed such attention. Returned it by stroking his palms over her curves, licking the tender spot between her breasts, wrapping his arms around her waist and pulling her close...

Kuzara. The core of his matrix roiled, seeking to resume an easier shape. His mouth was dry, and his eyes felt like they might explode from the growing pain in his head. He had to expand, to release himself from the confines of this quadruped body. The pressure was something he could no longer deny, witness or no witness.

With a shake that rolled through his shoulders and down his spine into his legs, he let himself shift.

"What the…" Maise dropped the nubby thing and stepped backward until her legs bumped the low table behind her.

He knelt with both palms planted against the stainless steel surface. Sudsy water dripped down his arms and legs, and he glared at his clawed blue hands, trying to make them more human. He'd transformed into his Fogarian body, an adult version of the one he'd grown up using, and was powerless at the moment to shift to a less familiar form.

"Help me," he said, staring downward at the table. If he spoke directly to her, she'd see his fangs, and he wasn't certain how she'd respond to that.

Maise hesitated only a heartbeat. "What can I do?"

"Water." His mouth felt dry, and it was the first thing he thought to ask for.

He snuck a glance as she hurried over to a desk where a monitor and keyboard were nearly buried in papers. She bent to open a small cube beneath it and returned with a plastic bottle. Uncapping it, she held it out. "Here."

He lifted a hand to take it and nearly fell on his face as his other palm skidded across the soapy table.

She reached out and caught his shoulder, helping him stay upright. She withdrew just as quickly, her uncertainty clashing against his Iki'i.

"Thank you," he said, still not looking at her as he settled back on his heels and tipped the bottle against his lips. The cool liquid burned all the way down his parched throat.

From the corner of his eye, he saw her attention fall to his lap and realized his genitalia were completely exposed. Luckily, the Fogarians were similar to humans in overall anatomy. But her interest made his cock stir.

She made a choked noise and her golden skin flushed russet. Grabbing a nearby cloth, she clutched it over her half-clothed torso, then pointed to a hose nozzle at the head of the table. "You can rinse off if you want." She grabbed another handful of cloths. "And here are towels."

Disliking the way his hand shook in front of her, he reached for the nozzle. He felt woozy, unbalanced. He wanted her to see him as strong and in command. Squeezing the handle released a warm spray, but his exhaustion was too much. He dropped the nozzle, letting it swing back against the pipe with a clang, and fell forward onto one hand.

"Shit," she breathed and stepped forward.

Warm water sluiced over his shoulders and back. He closed his eyes as her fingers threaded the back of his curly hair and brushed along his thick sideburns with the spray, helping remove the soapy residue.

She set the nozzle back in its holder and draped a towel over his shoulders, rubbing gently to dry him off. Her touch was comforting. Even more so was her concern for him as she helped him step off the table and wrap a towel around his waist.

"Please tell me what's going on," she said. Though her voice and actions seemed calm, he sensed her inner turmoil, the trembling uncertainty of facing the unknown. He had to admire her strength.

He'd intended to slip away when her back was turned, and hadn't bothered to fabricate a cover story, but since it was obvious that he'd need to spend a little more time with her while he recovered, he knew he had to come up with something fast—if she learned he was a smuggler, she'd turn him in.

Stalling for time, he answered, "My name's Iroth."

"Okay, Iroth. We need to get you to a doctor."

"No. Human doctors can't help me. Please, I'm in danger. No one can know I'm here."

She frowned. "Why?"

He expected her to be wary, suspicious. But his Iki'i only sensed confusion and concern. A desire to tell her the truth infused him.

But he buttoned down the urge. No matter how understanding she seemed, once she understood what he was, she'd turn on him, just like everyone else. Most *burendos* were detected early and eradicated—he'd survived by being quick on his feet. And he had to do that now if he wanted to keep surviving.

He concentrated hard on retracting his pointed teeth, making his Fogarian face as human as possible before meeting her gaze. He'd heard the woman who interviewed Maise say that there'd been an assassination attempt on the prince. Perhaps he could use that information to keep her silent. "I was a decoy for the prince. He suspected an assassination attempt might happen."

Her marvelously green eyes widened. "Why didn't you come forward during the investigation?"

"I was instructed not to reveal my true identity to anyone," he lied. "The royal family doesn't know who to trust."

She covered her mouth, her distress palpable even without his Iki'i. "My friend Lora is helping one of his bodyguards. Do you think she's in danger?"

He shook his head. "I'm sure she's fine as long as she doesn't know anything that might compromise the prince."

Nodding, she offered him another towel.

He wrapped it around his waist, marveling at the ease of this conversation. He couldn't recall ever meeting anyone as inherently trusting, as innately *good,* as this human female. Guilt ebbed up his spine, a feeling he hadn't felt in a very long time.

But if he wanted to survive, he had no other choice but to deceive her. "I need a place to recover until I can get back to my ship."

She bit her bottom lip and nodded. "My apartment's upstairs. You can rest there for a while."

He let out a sigh of relief. "Thank you."

Leaning heavily on her shoulder, he exited the building and ascended an exterior staircase, clutching the towel around his waist. Her small quadruped followed close behind, satisfied the female had interpreted its signals.

They entered the domicile, and he collapsed onto a sofa, barely taking in the cluttered space. Maise offered him another drink and put a hand against his forehead.

He seldom got close enough to anyone to be touched, and his eyes drifted closed in satisfaction. It was hard to think of anything but her. He'd always taken for granted his natural Kirenai resiliency. "You really need a doctor. Are you sure there isn't anyone we can call?"

He shook his head and repeated, "No one can know I'm alive."

Sighing, she pulled a blanket from the back of the cushions behind him and tucked the edges around his body. "I can't believe I'm doing this." She smiled wryly. "Don't you dare die on my couch."

He smiled back, gratified that she could find irony in the situation. Then he closed his eyes and hoped he wouldn't wake in a royal military brig.

4

*E*ver since Mom started calling her a dog whisperer, Maise had been inclined to help any living thing; dogs, birds, even people. And one thing was sure—this alien needed her help.

She watched him sleep on her couch for a long time. It was difficult to believe he'd looked like a Great Dane less than an hour ago. If she hadn't seen him transform before her very eyes, she wouldn't have believed it herself.

At the moment, he didn't look at all dog-like. His features were broader than a human's and slightly flattened, and his dark blue facial hair reminded her of photos of her father back in the seventies when bushy sideburns were in style. Although his hands each had five fingers, his fingernails were curved and sharp like claws, and he had thick, fur-like hair on the backs of his knuckles.

Her attention drifted lower over the lap blanket that barely covered his naked legs and towel-wrapped hips, remembering other parts of his anatomy she'd glimpsed. The very thick, dark blue mat of hair on his chest tapered toward his crotch, and she could still envision the massive shaft of his cock stirring to life under her gaze. Her body flushed as she realized he'd seen her nearly naked as well. A brief fantasy of what it might've been like to press their bodies together flitted across her mind.

She shook off the image, wondering what was wrong with her. She rarely liked hairy men, and this guy—no, this *alien*—had what looked like a pelt on portions of his body. Not to mention he'd been a dog not so very long ago. She shouldn't find him remotely attractive. Maybe it was because he smelled so damn good? The scent of men's cologne still hovered around him, a pleasing smell like musky pine that reminded her of walks in the woods. She'd always found good quality men's cologne a turn on.

Sighing, she tiptoed back to her bedroom, closed the door, and threw on a pair of leggings and a long tee shirt. Then she sat on the edge of the bed, staring at the nearest travel poster on her wall. What if he didn't get better? What if he died? She recalled with horrifying clarity the way her date had turned into gooey blue gel. She had to help Iroth before he got worse, while he still had a body to heal.

But she had no clue why he might be sick or if it was even related to what had happened to the others. She needed more information. *Lora's working with an alien.* Perhaps her friend could offer information that would help. Maise would simply need to be careful not to let anything slip about the alien on her couch in case the NSA had tapped their phones. She dialed Lora's cell.

"You've reached Officer Lora Griffin with the Springfield Police Department. Leave me a message and I'll get back to you."

Maise sighed and hung up. Lora was most likely still at the crime scene. She'd ring back as soon as she had a chance.

Looking around for Bixby, Maise realized the dog had stayed with Iroth. The sheltie was a lot like her, interested in people and driven to help. They'd met when Bixby's service animal trainer had brought the dog in for grooming. A service animal needed to stay focused on her owner, but every new person who walked in the door had garnered Bixby's attention. "I just can't train it out of her," the trainer complained. "She loves people too much. I think I'm going to have to list her for adoption."

"I'll take her," Maise offered, then cringed over the adoption cost. But she'd pulled together the money. All she knew was that she and Bixby understood each other on a fundamental level. They'd been constant companions ever since.

It made sense that Bixby wanted to help the alien as badly as Maise did. Either that, or the sheltie had a crush on the Great Dane.

Girl, same. That thought made Maise smirk, but she sobered quickly. A body double for a prince seemed like the perfect job for an alien who could change shape—until someone tried to assassinate him. Did Iroth look like the prince now, or was he in his own shape? "So weird," she muttered.

She rose from the bed and cracked open the door just as her phone began to cluck like a mother hen. Quickly closing the door again, she answered, "Hi, Mom."

"Darling, did I leave my jacket at your house?"

Mom hadn't been to her apartment above Yappy Hour in over a year. Her progressing dementia made seeing the veterinary clinic she'd run for twenty years now relegated to pet grooming and boarding, no matter how often Maise assured her it was temporary.

Maise quickly texted her Dad—*On phone with Mom. She's confused.*—while still talking to her mom. "Are you and Dad going somewhere?"

"It's Sunday, Maise." The reproach in her mother's voice was clear. "Church starts in an hour and I'm supposed to do the reading. That's why I need my jacket."

She's dressing for church, she texted. "Ok, I'll look around for it. Have you eaten breakfast?"

There was a pause as Mom considered. "I don't remember."

Maise heard Dad's indistinct rumble in the background, and Mom replied to him, "I'll be there in a minute." Her voice once more returned to the phone. "What did you need, darling?"

"You answered my question." Deflecting her had been easy for once. "Thanks, Mom. Love you."

"I love you too."

As she hung up, Maise bit her lip and stared at her phone. "She's getting worse." Dad could not take care of her on his own forever.

But that was a problem for another day. Right now, there was an alien on her couch who needed help. She dialed Lora again and still got her voicemail. Hanging up, she texted, *call me,* and grabbed a blanket from her bed before returning to the living room.

Bixby watched from where she was curled up on the floor near Iroth's head. The tip of her tail wagged slightly in greeting.

"Good dog." Maise lay the bigger blanket on top of the small lap blanket, wishing she could take his temperature or other vitals to understand what might be wrong. But she didn't know what a normal temp would be for an alien, let alone pulse rate or respiration. He seemed peaceful enough lying there.

She put the back of her hand against his forehead. As before, he felt slightly feverish compared to a human, but that could be normal.

For now, she set the water bottle within his reach, rubbed behind Bixby's ears, and retrieved her notes from her toxicology class. One of the top reasons pets needed urgent care was because they'd eaten something poisonous. Perhaps she'd find something useful for Iroth in her notes.

She kicked up the footstool on her recliner and began reading. Her eyes were bleary, though, and her attention kept drifting to the couch. She watched his chest move slowly up and down, reassured by its steadiness. Slowly, her eyes drifted closed.

5

*J*roth battled fevered dreams of himself wearing traditional Kirenai *happa* bark armor and being pursued by a giant, growling *nezumi*. Of shifting and shifting and shifting. All while being watched by a pair of green eyes. In between, he woke to water against his lips. A female's gentle hands and soothing words.

He didn't know how long he lay there, fighting to keep his matrix cohesive, but he finally cracked open his lids and kept them open.

Sunlight slanted through the slats covering a nearby window, low on the horizon, and it took several minutes to remember where he was. On the wall facing him hung a media screen with multiple wires snaking down to small electronics on a low table below. A piece of plush furniture suited for a single person sat beside him. Another wall held a set of shelves overflowing with books, and on the opposite side of the room four chairs made of what looked like sticks surrounded a small table scattered with more books and papers.

He pushed the blanket aside and sat up. He felt like *kuzara*, but the pounding in his head seemed to have receded. A female's scent hovered around him, making his cock stir despite his weakened state. *Maise*. The human had placed an extra blanket over him at some point, and a bottle of water waited on the floor beside the couch. He drained it before attempting to stand.

Maise's quadruped, Bixby, rose to greet him, bumping her muzzle beneath his palm. The dog was as nurturing as the human, and he could sense she wanted approval, so he patted the fur between her pointed ears. Was it morning or evening? It didn't matter. It was time for him to leave.

Then he realized he couldn't. The moment he left, Maise would call the authorities. Which left him in an unfortunate position. He needed everyone to believe he'd died with the others. To keep his secret, he had to silence her. He wasn't a killer, which left him only one option—kidnap her. *She'll be worth a lot of money on the black market.*

A fierce protectiveness rose inside him at the thought. Humans were traded on the galactic black market as breeders, and Maise deserved better. She'd rescued him, sheltered him without hesitation, probably saved his life. But what the *kuzara* was he going to do with her if not sell her?

He'd come up with something later. Right now, he had to figure out how to take her with him.

The domicile appeared to extend beyond this room, so he padded toward the hallway, the nappy fabric beneath his feet reminding him of the moss on Kirenai Prime. Not that he'd spent much time there, but when he'd visited, he'd always enjoyed the lushness of his species' home world. His mother's planet, the one of his early youth, had been one of rocks and lichen.

He reached the kitchen, and the room seemed to spin around him, forcing him to pause with one arm against a cupboard. Bixby nosed his hand as if trying to tell him something, and he realized he was starving. Whatever had been wrong with him had sapped his strength. He would require sustenance to reach his ship.

But many species shared communal space, and he didn't want any surprises; he couldn't eat until he'd examined the rest of the domicile.

Passing the kitchen, he headed toward two open doors at the end of the hall. The first was a bedroom lit by filtered light from a curtained window. A large mattress took up most of the space, and a dresser against the far with a drawer hanging open. Maise lay on top of the covers, face relaxed in sleep and one hand clasped over the top of a notebook.

He stood in the doorway, admiring her finely defined nose adorned with a sparkling gem at the crease of one nostril, strong eyebrows, and perfectly fanned crescents of eyelashes. He yearned to run a finger along the seam between her full lips, to see if they were as soft as he imagined. His gaze drifted down to where her nipples jutted like beacons against the thin fabric of her pale yellow shirt. Shapely legs ended with bare feet, toenails painted a deep burgundy.

Every aspect of her was breathtaking, and his cock stirred against the rough fabric of the towel around his waist. He looked down, suddenly self-conscious about his Fogarian body. His most naturally assumed form was also the one he most avoided. It had too many memories attached. And while Maise had been curious about him, he couldn't recall feeling attraction.

His throat tightened as he realized he wanted her to desire him. *It would make it easier to get her to my ship.*

Peeking into the other open door, he recognized the windowless room as a lavatory. He searched the nearby wall for atmospheric controls and found a pair of simple toggles that activated a light and a fan. A wide mirror spanned the wall behind the sink.

He quickly stepped inside and closed the door before Bixby could follow. The animal was intelligent, and Iroth preferred to make adjustments to his form in private. He was immediately struck by the image of his father looking back at him: flat features, thick sideburns, heavy brow. He grimaced and leaned closer to the mirror, noticing that his teeth were blunt, more like a human's than a Fogarian's. At least he'd managed to hide his fangs.

Concentrating, he retracted his bushy sideburns and the pelt covering his chest, leaving only a cap of thick hair over his scalp. He also changed his claws to flattened fingernails. He leaned heavily on the countertop, panting. The effort of changing had almost been too much to handle. But now when he looked at himself, he might pass for human—except for his color. His skin was still a deep teal, with dark blue hair and eyes.

He looked down at the towel that parted below his hips, showing off one of his muscled thighs. He often created clothing with his disguises, finding it easier to alter them than remove them if he had to make a quick change. But he'd barely been able to make himself look somewhat human. Clothing was out of the question at the moment.

A vibrant pink robe hung from a hook on the back of the door. It smelled of Maise as strongly as the blanket she'd thrown over him. Leaving the towel on underneath, he forced his arms into the robes' sleeves and tied the sash. The garment was too small to close across his chest, but it covered his lower half better than the towel.

When he opened the door, Bixby stood waiting, her tail sweeping back and forth. Why was this quadruped so interested in him? Shouldn't she be paying attention to Maise? He edged around her and headed toward the kitchen. Once he'd eaten something, he'd feel better.

He opened a large humming cupboard that looked different from the rest and discovered cold food storage. Perfect. The most familiar items would be whole foods that required chilling rather than the packaged, shelf-stable items likely to be in the cupboards. He picked up a clear plastic rectangle and pried open the lid, revealing what he believed might be vegetable matter mixed with spices. A bottle of red paste smelled tangy, and another bottle held the bright red juice of a sour fruit. A tall rectangular carton appeared to hold the mammary excretion of some animal. He opened a cellulose carton and discovered two rows of white eggs and sighed with relief. Eggs were a classic food throughout the galaxy, with variations in flavor and texture.

He set the carton on the counter, wondering what stage of development they were in. He preferred his eggs cooked and investigated the appliances until he discovered one with coils that produced heat. There were several metal pans in a nearby cupboard, so he set one to heating.

Then he noticed Bixby standing expectantly in front of a pair of empty metal bowls. She met his gaze and did a small dance on her four paws, then froze again next to the bowls, waiting.

He smiled despite himself. Her dance was entertaining. Sensing she was thirsty, he picked up one bowl and filled it at the sink. She lapped at the water, gratitude thrumming against his Iki'i. He felt like a child again, hand-feeding his baby *nezumi*. He clamped down the memory and turned back to the heating pan. *Do not get attached*. Attachment led to trust, and trust led to betrayal, even if that betrayal only meant one of them ended up on the dinner table.

Cracking an egg into the pan, he was delighted to discover it was in a pre-fertilization stage of development, with a golden yolk and delicate albumen that turned white when heated. He cracked several more, stirring slightly and adding some sodium chloride crystals he'd located in a shaker nearby. He was just sliding the eggs onto a ceramic plate when a voice made him jump.

"Good morning." Maise stood next to the cold storage unit, smiling at him. Relief saturated the space around her, along with mild humor as she took in the pink robe. Then her eyes lifted to his face and a flood of attraction rushed toward him. "You shaved."

His own satisfaction made him smile back. She liked the changes to his form. He held out the plate. "Would you care for some eggs?"

"Mm, that would be lovely. Thank you. Take them to the table and I'll bring plates."

Bixby did her little dance again, hunger pricking his Iki'i. He looked at the eggs, not wanting to share. "Your pet is hungry, too."

Maise laughed and opened a lower cupboard next to Bixby's dishes. "I'm sure she is. Sorry girl, no eggs for you. Bixby gets kibble."

He couldn't help but stare at Maise's nicely rounded backside as she poured something from a bag into the empty dish, filling the small kitchen with a tinging sound. He loved watching her move, feeling the comfort she exuded, the self-confidence in her own space. The way she welcomed him into it made him happy.

A sudden wave of vertigo swept through him, and he nearly dropped the plate.

She grabbed it and set it on the counter behind him. "Are you okay? Go sit down. I'll bring things over."

He nodded, ashamed of his weakness. Her concern for him was like a heavy blanket wrapping around his shoulders; a welcome weight that made him want to curl up and sleep again. Yet at the same time, he was guiltily forming a plan to use Maise's compassion to get her onto his ship. Regret burning his throat, he went to the chairs and sat.

She followed close behind and shoved aside papers and books to make room for the dishes. "Sorry for the mess. I've been studying for my exams."

"What sort of exams?"

"I'm almost finished with veterinary school. I want to open my own practice downstairs." She divided the eggs onto their plates and sprinkled tiny black specks over hers before taking a bite. "Mm, good eggs."

He took a bite of his own, satisfied by the creamy texture and rich flavor. They chatted about what she was learning. He'd never finished school, and found her many years of dedication to study intriguing. "All of this so you can take care of species that are not your own?"

She shrugged. "I grew up helping Mom run the clinic. I think I spent more time with the dogs than with my family. Mom really wanted—wants—me to become a vet."

He nodded, sensing in her a bitterness that matched his feelings about his own family. "I think I understand."

They finished their eggs, and she rose. "Do you want more?"

He put his hand over hers, startled by a jolt of awareness at the feel of her soft skin under his palm. "No, thank you. But I need to ask for your help again. I must inform the prince about what I know." He hated himself for what he was about to do, but he had no other choice. "Will you take me to my ship?"

She frowned and sat back down. "Of course. Where is it?"

"Near the outskirts of your city. Hidden in the trees near an enormous building that bellows foul-smelling steam."

"The pulp mill." She nodded. "I can drive you there, no problem. Are you certain you're well enough to leave?"

"It doesn't matter. I must leave Earth immediately. I know who was behind the assassination attempt." He rubbed his thumb over the back of her knuckles. His Iki'i felt her attraction for him like a caress. He had a momentary fantasy of leaning forward and tasting her lips. Cupping the swell of her breast—

The inner coil of his matrix spasmed and pulsed, as if on the verge of losing cohesion. He pulled his hand from hers, worried he might collapse into his resting state right before her eyes. "I need to leave as soon as possible."

Her lips thinned and regret knotted the space between them. She picked up the dishes. "I'll dig up some clothes for you and we can go."

As she returned to the kitchen, he made a point of leaning down to pet Bixby so he wouldn't be tempted to watch the sway of Maise's hips.

6

aise drove Iroth to the pulp mill and parked just inside the fence around the parking lot. Thankfully, the plant's workers were in the middle of a shift and there was no one standing around the scattered parked cars. She looked over at the passenger seat. Iroth had exchanged her hot pink robe for an old, paint-splattered flannel shirt and sweats that strained around his thickly muscled arms and thighs. A black baseball cap with the Yappy Hour logo on the front and sunglasses shaded his face. It seemed the tall blue alien could look sexy no matter what he was wearing.

"Where do we go from here?" she asked.

"Through those trees." He indicated the woods on the other side of the fence, a line of vegetation that

47

followed the river to the right before rising into craggy foothills.

Over the past two days, she'd fretted over him, worrying that he might die at any moment. According to the news, not a single blue alien at the auction had survived. She hadn't been able to reach Lora or Georgie for advice and hated not knowing what to do to help him. She'd even toyed with the idea of calling the number the NSA agent had given her; social media was rife with fear about aliens coming to take revenge on humanity for the massacre, and Iroth was the only one who knew the truth about what had happened.

But she'd resisted, remembering how adamant he'd been that no one could know he was alive.

When she'd discovered him making breakfast in her kitchen, she'd been overjoyed. And despite her determination to help him report back to the prince, she wondered where things might've gone if he didn't have to leave right now. He was such a good listener, and every time he touched her, she felt a little thrill of attraction. After he was gone, she'd be fantasizing for weeks—maybe months—about being holed up in her apartment with a hot blue alien.

You need to get back to class so you can graduate, she reminded herself. Though, to be fair, she wasn't looking forward to tying herself to a vet clinic for the rest of her life. It'd been fine for Mom, but Maise had always dreamed of travel. And after this bit of excitement, the course of her life seemed even more boring.

Iroth got out of the car and leaned on the mirror as if about to fall over.

Worry flared in her gut, and she hurried to his side, stuffing her keys into the front pocket of her hoodie.

He met her gaze, his turquoise eyes full of strain. "I wasn't going to ask, but would you mind helping me walk the rest of the way? It isn't far."

She sighed, furrowing her brow. "I sure hope you know what you're doing. Stay here a sec so I can let Bixby out."

Opening the back of the Jeep, she let the sheltie hop down, opting not to use a leash since there was no one around to complain. The dog waited patiently as Maise put one shoulder under Iroth's arm, then trotted along beside them as they walked through the gate toward the trees.

Iroth was barefoot, since none of her shoes would fit him, and he stepped carefully across the uneven ground. His cologne had been intriguing from the moment she'd met him, but for some reason now it was downright sexy. *Maybe because he'd shaved?* The longer she knew him, the more attractive he seemed. She could even swear he was taller than she first remembered.

They followed a dry creek bed, and she adjusted her arm around his waist to help him down the incline, her insides fluttering as her fingers contacted the muscle peeking from beneath the too-small shirt.

He paused when they reached a clearing, tightening his arm around her shoulders. "Here we are."

She liked his arm around her, adding it to her fantasy repertoire as she gripped his waist and looked around at the grass and weeds. Several yards away, Bixby was pacing and sniffing the ground. "Where's your ship?"

Iroth let go of her shoulders and tapped a spot on his wrist, speaking in a language she didn't understand. The air in the middle of the clearing shimmered, and something that looked like a purple butterfly chrysalis appeared.

She gasped.

The thing was about the size of a city bus and rested with the pointed end slightly elevated above its bulbous base. One edge unfolded like a petal, forming a ramp to the ground, and she realized it didn't look like a chrysalis so much as a rosebud.

He smiled, once again leaning on her shoulder. "Help me up the ramp."

Her heart thudded hard against her breastbone. She was looking at a real live space ship. Helping a real live alien.

Bixby sniffed the ramp, then trotted ahead. Maise stared in awe at the delicately veined floor and walls as they ascended the incline.

Inside the cramped space, a pedestal rose from the floor in the center in the same lavender-colored material as everything else. The entire interior seemed to glow with ambient light rather than from overhead fixtures. A row of four seats was molded into one wall. She touched the arm of one, rubbing the leathery texture. "Everything looks organic—made of leaves or something."

"You're correct." He moved to a waist high console and ran his fingers over its bumpy surface. Multicolored lights appeared among the bumps, and a screen on one wall lit up to show the trees outside. "Most advanced technology has a biological component."

No one was ever going to believe her when she told them about this. She had to take pictures. But when she searched her pockets for her phone, she remembered she'd left it charging by her bed. *Crap.*

The floor vibrated beneath her feet, as if he'd started the engine, and she knew it was time for her to go. Biting her lip, she put a hand on his arm. "Guess this is where we say goodbye." She didn't know why, but she felt sad thinking she'd never see him again. "If you ever visit Earth again, look me up, okay?"

He turned to her and pointed to the seats, his face an unreadable mask. "Please sit over there."

A wave of doubt swept over her. She turned toward the door and discovered Bixby pacing the spot where the opening had been. Maise spun to face Iroth. "What's going on? You need to let us off!"

His features remained calm, one hand resting on the bumpy console. "I'm sorry that I must do this. But if you don't sit down, I'll be forced to restrain you."

She stuck her hand into her hoodie pocket and gripped her keys, as Lora had taught them in self-defense class. "Go ahead and try. You can barely stand up!" But even as she said it, she realized how stupid she'd been. He'd been faking his illness. This was the oldest serial killer trick in the book, and she'd fallen for it. The only thing that might've worked better was if he'd claimed to have a sick puppy on board. And escaping from an alien space ship was going to be a lot more difficult than escaping some creeper's abduction van. "You tricked me."

"Yes, and I deeply regret it. Now sit."

She glanced at Bixby, who now lay against the wall, a soft whine coming from her throat as if begging to be let out. *So much for canine protection.* Maise hated the tears filming her vision. "But we rescued you. Why are you hurting us?"

"I will not hurt you. But if I leave you here, you'll tell the authorities. Everyone must think I died along with the others."

"I won't tell, I swear." She thought of the various messages she'd left for Lora, the vague hints that something weird was going on.

His eyes were like stone. "I'd like to believe that, but I know better."

Her throat tightened with another suspicion. "Are you the assassin?"

He turned his attention to the console. "No, but it doesn't matter. I was there."

Gritting her teeth, she reached for bumps and lights, hitting as many as she could and praying the door would open.

"Stop." He grabbed her wrist and grimaced, flashing pointed teeth.

She stumbled backward, heart stuttering in terror. Where had those come from?

Still holding her wrist, he advanced a step. "Sit."

Her gaze went to her wrist, where his fingers once more ended in claws instead of fingernails. It had all been a disguise. A human-like façade to make her feel comfortable. Even his face had once more sprouted hair, though it was more like human stubble than the bushy sideburns he'd had the first time.

Trembling, she fell back into a seat. The cushioning enveloped her like a bean bag gone wrong, suctioning around her. She thrashed, but it refused to let her go. On the screen, she saw Lora appear in the clearing with Pepper tugging on a leash.

"Lora!" she screamed.

But it was too late. All she could do was watch as the ground fell away beneath them.

7

*T*roth cloaked the shuttle and hurtled into orbit toward his ship, sending an encrypted message to Zhinko, his ship's AI, that he was on the way. He'd been on the surface too long, and the crystals used for the cloaking device were nearly spent. Keeping the cloak operational while moving would use even more, and he hoped there was enough to hide the shuttle until they reached his ship.

As they exited the atmosphere into the inky void of space, his gut churned with regret about tricking Maise, but it wasn't like he had a choice. No one could know he'd survived. It didn't matter that he'd never hired himself out for assassinations—his name was on the IDA guest list. He'd be front and center of the galaxy's most wanted boards if anyone discovered he'd survived the massacre, because everyone would assume a *burendo* was to blame. Just like when he was nine and got blamed for stealing lunches at school or his adolescence when he'd been invited to a party and got accused of forcing himself on a girl.

He synchronized the shuttle controls with his ship's AI and let the computer take over guidance into the cargo bay, the horrific memory still clawing inside of him. He'd kissed that girl once that night in a game. His very first kiss. But someone else had done more than kiss her. And no amount of words from him would convince the authorities it hadn't been him.

Worse, even his parents had doubts. Their disappointment weighed heavier than anything he'd ever imagined possible. "It doesn't matter if you did it or not, Iroth," his father had said as they left the juvenile detainment unit. "You were there, which makes you guilty."

Right after that, his family had moved. Again. It had felt like hopelessness took up most of the room in their suitcases. That was the moment he'd decided that if he was going to be blamed for breaking the rules, he no longer needed to follow them.

Iroth Sanoko needed to wink out of existence, and so did Maise. She knew his name, what he looked like in his most familiar form, even what he smelled like; all things that might be used to track him down before he could secure a new identity.

Ahead, the starlit void shimmered, and a shaft of light appeared as the ship's cargo bay doors opened. As the shuttle settled to the docking bay floor, his insides convulsed. He gripped one arm across his middle. Despite his long rest in Maise's domicile, he was not yet fully recovered. He needed time in his resting pod and possibly medication. He opened the shuttle's hatch and lowered the ramp.

Still cushioned in the jump seat, Maise looked ashen, lips pressed into a thin line. His Iki'i sensed her nausea, which wasn't helping with his own roiling insides. He closed off his senses before he embarrassed himself by vomiting breakfast. "I'm sorry the ride was rough. The cloaking device interferes with the shuttle's stabilizers. But we've reached my ship now, and I think you'll find it quite comfortable."

Although the circumstances weren't ideal, he was excited to show her his domain. He'd worked for a long time to afford a small luxury liner of his own, and longer still to outfit it with the latest FTL drives, black market cloaking technology, and an AI bondservant. The AI had been the best investment of all, able to care for the ship and keep it from being marked for salvage if Iroth had to be away for extended jobs. The vessel was Iroth's sanctuary.

Releasing Maise from her jump seat, he held out a hand to help her stand.

She batted it away and struggled to rise on her own. "Don't touch me, asshole."

He sighed, unable to deny her anger.

Zhinko's even tenor voice floated up the ramp. "Welcome back, Captain."

Stepping to the open hatch, he spotted the small, black, egg-shaped module that acted as Zhinko's hands on board the ship hovering at the base of the ramp.

"You were gone longer than expected," Zhinko said. "Would you like me to prepare a meal for you and the female?"

"Not right now," Iroth said. "I need my resting pod. Will you please ready it for diagnostic protocols?"

"Of course, Captain." The module backed away but remained hovering nearby, ready to assist with other tasks while its main ship processors prepared the resting pod in the medical bay.

Maise still stood at the top of the ramp, one white-knuckled hand gripping the edge of the hatch opening. Bixby sat at her feet, leaning into Maise's leg and looking upward as if awaiting instructions. Both of them pulsed with uncertainty, though Maise was also generating fear and anger. "Please, Iroth. Take us home. You don't want to do this.He understood her desperation, but there was no going back now. At least he could make her as comfortable as possible. "I've reserved the best room for you." He patted his thigh in invitation, as she'd done when they'd first met. "Come this way."

Bixby took a few steps down the ramp, then turned back to Maise as if to ask if she was coming.

Maise remained planted at the shuttle doorway. "I'm not your dog, and I don't respond to hand signals." She patted her leg, calling Bixby back to her side. "Will you please at least let me call my family? If you tell us how much you want, we'll try to come up with the money."

His throat grew tight. "Your family can provide nothing I need." He marched up the ramp and gripped her arm, using all his will to transform his claws into blunt nails. "It will be okay. Come with me now."

"Ow!" Maise tried to pull away. "You're hurting me."

Bixby growled, and Iroth glanced at the beast with surprise. She had her feet planted wide and was exposing her teeth. It was the first sign of aggression he'd sensed from her, and although the emotion was directed at him, he approved. He'd use his fangs and claws to defend Maise if she was threatened as well.

He let go of her arm and raised both palms. He'd wanted to show her the room himself rather than leaving it to Zhinko, but the instability in his matrix was growing more insistent. Interstitial fluid leaked from his pores like sweat. "I didn't mean to hurt you. Perhaps it would be better if I allowed my bondservant to escort you." Stepping back, he said. "Zhinko, please settle our guests in my private quarters."

The black egg floated forward. "There is no need to use your personal quarters, Captain. I have prepared one of the other rooms in anticipation of our cargo."

The other rooms on the ship were adequate lodging, but were intended for bondservants, with a shared lavatory and no exterior view screens. "My quarters, Zhinko. And give them any luxury they desire, but no access to core systems, communications, or the shuttle."

"Understood, Captain."

"What's going on?" Maise asked. "What are you saying?"

He remembered then that she didn't have a universal translator. He'd have to pick one up for her as soon as he got a chance. "Zhinko, please access universal translation file 86LF7 and introduce yourself."

The AI rotated in a circle, as if to face the newcomers. "Greetings, Maise and Bixby. Welcome on board," Zhinko said in Maise's native tongue. "My name is Zhinko, and I am honored to serve your needs. If you will allow me, I will show you to your accommodations now. If you are hungry, we have a fully outfitted galley and I would be delighted to prepare an excellent meal for you."

As Zhinko was speaking, Bixby trotted the rest of the way down the ramp to circle beneath the AI, looking up with her tongue lolling from one side of her mouth.

Reassured that at least Bixby would be happy, Iroth backed down the ramp while speaking to Maise. "You're free to explore anywhere except the lower level. Engineering's down there, and you could get hurt."

With that, he turned and strode toward the medical bay. It felt as if his bones would soon refuse to hold him upright, and a blue haze was sliding over his vision. He only hoped he made it to his resting pod before Maise saw him collapse.

8

Maise followed the thing that looked like a black floating egg away from the shuttle and through a door into a narrow purple hallway. Bixby trotted just behind her, content as usual. The dog's protective response when Iroth had grabbed Maise's arm had been short-lived, but that was to be expected—Bixby didn't have a suspicious bone in her body.

Just like me, thought Maise with disgust. And look where that got them.

"Can I make a phone call?" she asked the egg's back—assuming the thing even had a back. Or a front, for that matter. "I should let my parents know where I am, and I have a test tomorrow that I need to reschedule—"

"I'm sorry, but the captain has instructed me to restrict your access to the communication system. Is there something else I can provide for you?"

"How about a shuttle back home?" muttered Maise, knowing it was a futile request.

"Unfortunately, the shuttle and the ship's core systems are also prohibited," the egg answered as a panel in the hallway slid open to reveal a large room with a low bed covered by a deep red coverlet. An enormous window over the head of the bed looked out at velvet blackness and twinkling stars.

A moment of vertigo rocked Maise, and she put out a hand to support herself against the doorframe. *Holy crap, I'm actually in outer space.*

Bixby stopped moving as well, pressing her warm, furry flank comfortingly against Maise's leg. A wet nose nudged Maise's free hand.

Maise rubbed between the dog's ears, grounding herself in the familiar sensation. At least the room was nice, not some serial killer hole in the ground. She stepped slowly inside. "What does Iroth intend to do with me?" she asked the egg.

"He is under contract to deliver a human female to a client in the Pudari asteroid belt."

Icy dread flooded Maise. He intended to sell her? To who? And why? "He has no right! I'm not a slave, and he doesn't own me."

"You will have to address that with the captain. I am merely here to serve. He obviously considers you a prime specimen, however. I have never seen him offer his personal quarters for a passenger."

She glanced around at the artwork decorating the shelves and walls. A trio of red and violet statues that looked like they were covered in feathers sat in an alcove next to what might be a desk, and a painting of a burning red sunset between looming dark rocks resembling clawed fingers hung on the wall. Smaller figurines and artifacts lay scattered among the other shelves.

"These are his personal quarters?" she asked, wondering if he planned on sleeping here, too; just because he planned to sell her didn't mean he didn't also intend to sample the goods.

"Indeed. Would you like to see our selection of virtual entertainment options?"

No way was she going to kick back and watch a movie right now. She needed to find a way off this ship while there might still be a chance of reaching Earth. "Are there other crew members on board?"

"Captain Iroth and I are the only crew."

Maise sighed. So much for appealing to the mercy of a crew member. She doubted there was much she could say to a robot egg to convince it to set her free. *Perhaps I can change Iroth's mind.* All Maise needed was time and interaction to make him change his mind.

"Where's Iroth?" she asked. "I want to speak with him."

"He's in his resting pod recovering. It seems he encountered something poisonous on your planet and requires a detoxification protocol."

"Poison." That made sense, considering how many aliens had been affected. They wouldn't have realized they were eating or drinking poison until they all got sick. *Or died.* Her heart hammered against her ribs as another thought occurred to her. "What happens to me if Iroth dies?"

The egg rotated slowly. "I do not believe he has made provisions for your contract in the event of his death. I would be honor bound to deliver you to our client in his stead."

She gulped. Was there no way out of this damn situation? "Will you please keep me informed about Iroth's recovery?"

"Absolutely." The egg bobbed as if performing a bow. "Might I suggest you join your companion and rest now? I will alert you when it is time for dinner."

She looked over to find Bixby had hopped onto the bed and now lay there with her eyes closed. "Traitor," she muttered and turned back to the egg. "All right. Thank you."

"Should you have questions, simply ask and I will assist you."

The egg floated through the door, which slid closed behind it.

Maise waited a few minutes, then approached the door, curious if she'd been locked inside. It slid open automatically at her approach.

The egg's voice floated through the room. "Did you think of something you need?"

"Oh," Maise flinched and looked around. The hallway outside was empty. *Of course there are cameras.* Good to know. But at least she wasn't locked in. Iroth had said she was free to explore. "I was just looking around."

"Very good."

Stepping back inside, Maise went to the desk. If these were Iroth's personal chambers, perhaps she'd discover something to help her convince him to take her home. She regretted not asking more questions about him during breakfast this morning. He'd been such a good listener, and she'd done nothing but talk about herself. *Stupid me.*

She touched the desktop, and a virtual screen winked to life above it. Symbols blinked on the screen, none of them decipherable. She moved on to examine the other items scattered about the room.

The feathered statues were knee high looked more like red and purple six-legged crabs than birds. The shelves held figurines of alien creatures and other indecipherable shapes that seemed to be made of gemstones. A small box contained what looked like puzzle pieces, and a plant with tiny leaves shivered when she touched it, producing a strange harmonic note that brought Bixby to her side, tail wagging.

"I don't know what it is, either, Bixby." She touched it again, this time creating a discordant note. One entire branch trembled so violently, she thought it might fall off, so she decided she'd better not touch again.

She opened a door and discovered an opulent bathroom with surprisingly human looking fixtures. Besides a wide sink and commode, there was a shower with four spigots, and when she ran her hand across some bumps on the wall that looked like they might be controls, the shower heads turned on and a fruity smell filled the air.

Not in the mood to shower in fruit juice, she wandered back into the bedroom and frowned at the shelves. No clothing. No books. "Why aren't there any photos?"

The egg's familiar voice answered, "We have a selection of photos in the ship's database." The virtual screen on the desk began a slideshow of landscapes. "Is there a particular place you would like to see?"

"Computer, are you always listening?"

"I am Zhinko, the ship's onboard intelligence. It is my duty to anticipate the needs of everyone on board."

No chance of sneaking around and finding an escape, then. Which only left convincing Iroth to let her go. Maise moved to the desk and watched the images float by.

"Are there any pictures of people, Zhinko?"

"We keep a database of client photos. Would you like to see those?" What looked like alien mug shots began appearing on the screen. Bug eyes, green skin, slitted noses…

"Do you have an image of the client who bought me?"

The passing images settled on an alien that resembled a blue-scaled lizard. "Uragi Rhimono, a prominent member of the Senburu."

She shuddered, contemplating what a creature like that might want with a human female. "Do you know how much he paid for me?"

"I am not at liberty to discuss the captain's finances."

Of course not. "Do you have any personal photos? Like Iroth's family or friends."

The screen went dark. "There is only one historic image I am aware of in our database. It has no label."

"Show me, please."

The image of what Maise assumed was a family appeared on the screen; a blue man with bushy sideburns similar to Iroth's when he'd first appeared to her, a woman with fiery crimson hair and thick eyebrows, and a small, teal-skinned child between them, baring his pointed teeth in a smile. Behind them loomed craggy black rocks that rose like claws from the ground, as if ready to clamp down on the family's heads.

"Do you know where this picture was taken?"

"There is a ninety-eight-point-eight percent chance this was taken at the Tasigrad Spires on Fogaria."

She sat in the padded chair facing the desk. "Those must be his parents. Do you know anything about them?"

"No. Iroth does not speak of his family."

She looked closer at the child, wishing she knew more about him so she could build empathy. That was the only way she was going to convince him to let her go. But he had a family, and that would be a starting point. Next time they talked, she was going to be the one asking the questions.

9

Iroth couldn't find rest, despite the soothing feel of the regeneration fluid bathing his matrix. He'd been listening to the news while he recovered, and it turned out the *Khensei* toxin his diagnostics equipment had found in his system was the same one reported to have killed the guests at the auction.

"We are fortunate you avoided a lethal dose," Zhinko said. "I do not want to look for a new owner."

Unable to respond while in his resting state, Iroth silently agreed. Yet even surrounded by the news of the massacre, speculation about the prince's well-being, and the ongoing search for the assassin, all Iroth could think about was Maise.

She thinks I'm a monster. And not just for kidnapping her. When he'd reached the medical bay and seen his own face in the reflective glass above the counter, he'd been horrified to see that portions of his features had reverted to his Fogarian form, fangs and all. No wonder she'd been so terrified when he'd grabbed her arm. He needed to reassure her he wouldn't harm her. The problem was, he had no idea what he was going to do with her after that.

Zhinko floated into his field of vision next to the sparsely stocked medical shelves. "Your diagnostics indicate that your matrix is fully purged, Captain."

Iroth pulled himself into a basic humanoid structure and sat up. "How long was I in here?"

"You entered your resting pod approximately three jiros ago."

Three jiros was almost seven hours in Earth time. "What's Maise been doing?"

"She has been looking at photographs and having me translate information about Fogarian culture."

His stomach clenched. She was definitely trying to figure out what sort of monster he might be. He assembled his features into the human form he'd worn during their breakfast together.

"Would you like me to prepare a meal?" Zhinko asked in a hopeful tone. For some reason, the AI enjoyed cooking, even though it couldn't eat, and Iroth kept the ship well supplied with fresh foods.

Maise enjoyed our breakfast together earlier. Perhaps sharing another meal would bring back good feelings. "Yes, please. Make sure everything is safe for humans." Iroth recalled Maise's insistence that Bixby was to eat something special. "Do you have a recipe for kibble?"

"I would be delighted to find one, Captain."

Standing, Iroth glanced down at his naked body. The clothing Maise had loaned him lay in a crumpled heap on the floor between his resting pod and the med bay shelves. She'd found amusement in the items, but he didn't want to be seen as amusing. "Have the replicator prepare human clothing for me. Male specific, common, no ornamentation."

"Understood," said Zhinko. "Please be advised we are almost to the designated rendezvous point in the Pudari asteroid belt."

"What?" Iroth froze halfway out of his pod. He hadn't specified a trajectory when they'd fled Earth's orbit, so of course Zhinko had followed through with the original plan to deliver a female to their client. "Turn us around. Plot a course to the station near Sireta

Prime." He had contacts there that could forge a new identity for him.

"Would you like me to reserve a slot for the female with the bondservant broker on the station?"

"She's not for sale," Iroth clarified.

"I see." Zhinko bobbed as if thinking. "What about her companion?"

"No. They're both guests."

"Guests!" Lights flashed over Zhinko's dark surface. "How delightful. I will finally be able to use my hospitality programming as intended." The AI glided toward the door. "Oh, dear. Captain, I'm afraid our guests have ventured onto the engineering level. They will be here in—"

Maise and Bixby appeared in the doorway. Her eyes widened and her gaze slid down his chest to his groin before slinging back upwards. "We were wondering, um, how you were."

Kuzara. It seemed she was destined to see him naked. But at least she hadn't seen him in his resting state. Her dark curls were loose about her face, and dust smudged one cheek.

Putting both hands on her shoulders, he turned her around to guide her back the way she'd come and growled, "I told you to stay off this level."

As he followed close behind her, he realized he'd instinctively made himself taller than his usual size, tall enough to loom over her. Yet her nearness threatened to bowl him over. Her heady scent reminded him of musky *amai* wood incense, a popular aphrodisiac. His cock swelled, no longer in his control.

"How much are you selling me for?" She glanced over her shoulder at him. "I want a chance to counter offer."

He stopped walking. "Zhinko told you?"

She turned her head to look over her shoulder, keeping her gaze locked on his face. "Yes, and no matter what happens to me, I want to make sure Bixby's taken care of." Her voice remained firm, but her anxiety trembled against his Iki'i. "Don't let her end up on someone's dinner table or used for medical tests or something."

He stiffened. "I would never allow anyone to hurt Bixby. Or you."

"But you're selling me to a lizard man. How do you know he won't do something awful?"

"I'm not selling you."

She narrowed her eyes. "You're not?"

"I didn't buy you for our client. I don't own your contract."

She brightened. "So I can go home, then?"

"No."

Her attention slid once more to his groin where his shaft was now at full attention, impossible to ignore. Both unease and arousal spiked against his Iki'i. "If you're not selling me or taking me home, what are you going to do with me?"

He wasn't sure of the answer. All he knew was he wanted to cover her body with his, to feel the softness of her curves against his angles. He couldn't help himself. Stepping closer, he pressed her back against the narrow corridor. "You're mine."

Green eyes lifted to meet his, and she whispered, "You just told me I'm not your slave."

But she didn't squirm or try to run. Didn't push him away. Her breathing was fast and shallow, and her arousal was now strong enough to smell. She was conflicted, flustered, and he sensed that a nudge from him would tip her over into passion.

Inhaling deeply, he dropped his chin until their foreheads met and stared into her eyes. His erection bumped her stomach, the slight friction making him throb. Her breasts were two perfect pillows against his chest. Even her lips looked soft and utterly kissable. Slowly, he lowered his mouth toward hers—

"Did you not find the clothing to your liking, Captain?" Zhinko's voice jarred him back to the moment. "I can program something different if you prefer."

Iroth spun to face the hovering AI. It held a pair of blue denim pants and a plain white shirt dangling from one of its extendible arms.

"These will be fine, thank you." Iroth stepped quickly into the pants and pulled the stretchy shirt over his head.

"I'm going back to my room." Maise edged past him, her hands shoved into the front pocket of her shirt.

"I'm preparing kibble for dinner," Zhinko volunteered. "But I have been unable to decide on a beverage pairing. Do you have any suggestions, Maise?"

Maise stopped and frowned. "Kibble... For all of us?"

"Yes, at the captain's request."

Iroth shook his head. "I meant for Bixby, not us."

Zhinko laughed, a sound Iroth wasn't certain he'd ever heard before. "That explains why it was so difficult to find a recipe for human-grade kibble. I understand now. I will revise the menu accordingly."

The unit lifted toward the ceiling and zipped toward the galley.

Bixby pranced a few steps after it, then seemed to remember herself and returned to Maise's side, gazing down the hall with longing.

Maise edged farther down the hall toward the lift, shoulders hunched and hands still in her pockets. "Well." Her throat bobbed. "Thank you for thinking of Bixby."

"Anything I can do to make you more comfortable."

Nodding slightly, she turned and fled, the dog at her heels.

Iroth remained standing in the hallway until she disappeared around a corner. His body still trembled with lust. She'd felt it too, stoked his desire with her own. There could be no denying the magnetism between them, which would only increase the longer they were on the ship together. And *burendo* or not, he was still Kirenai, driven to pleasure a partner both in bed and out.

There was no reason either of them had to deny themselves. He just had to win her trust.

10

hat the hell is wrong with me? Maise wondered as she hurried back to her room. She'd almost kissed Iroth just now, even after all he'd done. She hadn't been here long enough to develop Stockholm Syndrome, had she? Her gaze roamed the desk and shelves full of curios before falling on the immense bed with its satiny red coverlet. Did he intend to join her here later?

You're mine. His words lingered at the back of her mind, making her pussy ache and her heart beat faster. She imagined herself falling back onto the mattress, the weight of Iroth's body between her legs. His breath against her skin. The subtle hint of his cologne filling her senses. The enormous erection that had been sandwiched against her belly instead pressing between her thighs…

She clutched her arms around herself. Her own response to Iroth scared her more than his obvious attraction to her. He was delicious in his human form, but he'd also appeared like a hairy beast with fangs. Who knew what other shapes he might take or which one was even real? *Banging a beast could be fun.* Holy shit, what was she even thinking?

As if sensing her distress, Bixby nudged her hand.

She looked down into the dog's warm brown eyes. *Kibble for dinner.* Beast or human, he was considerate enough to have thought of Bixby, which made him even more attractive. "I think I'm going crazy."

Closing her eyes, she tried to find a rational thought, one not wrapped up in feelings and intuition. Following her instincts had gotten her into this mess. If she wasn't careful, she'd end up doing something she regretted. *Think, Maise.*

Zhinko's voice entered the room. "Dinner will be ready soon. Would you like to freshen up? We have a wide selection of clothing designs in our replicator database." The screen above the desk began scrolling with images of clothing.

"You can just make clothes on demand?" She watched a designer pencil skirt and jacket set whisk by.

"Whatever you desire, however, our human clothing record is not yet complete. Earth's current fashion trends include many clothing items imprinted with words, which will take some time to compile."

"Can you make a pair of jeans and a simple turtle-neck sweater?" She figured that was classy without being sexy.

An alcove near the bathroom lit up. "Is this to your liking?"

Maise retrieved a pair of jeans and a deep purple sweater that felt soft as cashmere.

"If you prefer something else, simply ask and I will make it for you."

"This should be fine, thank you." She pulled her hair tie from her pocket and pulled her curls into a messy bun before stepping out of her old clothes and into the new. As she did, she watched the door, praying Iroth didn't show up while she was half naked.

An entire wall transformed into a mirror without warning. "Would you like to examine your appearance?"

Maise stiffened, momentarily startled, then regrouped and looked at her reflection. The jeans hugged her ass with precision, and the turtleneck enhanced her curves more than it ought to. *So much for not being sexy.* She considered requesting a baggier set, but then the door slid open.

Heart thundering, Maise spun, expecting to see Iroth. Instead, Zhinko's egg hovered there. "You look exquisite! It would be my honor to escort you to the dining room."

Maise couldn't help the smile that twitched her mouth. Was the AI offering to be her chaperone and protect her honor? She doubted the little egg could—or even would—stand up to Iroth if the need arose, but having him on her side felt nice. "I'd appreciate that."

She followed the AI around a bend into an open area with a massive view of the stars along one wall. A long table suitable for eight or ten people had been set for two—one at either end. Two stainless steel bowls rested on the floor near one chair, and Bixby immediately trotted over and began crunching on what Maise could only hope was the promised kibble.

Iroth stepped from behind a bar at one side of the room, carrying two martini glasses filled with something pink. He was even more handsome than before, looking like a casual, teal-blue James Bond in a white tee shirt that molded across his well-muscled chest and jeans slung low across his hips. He held out a glass. "Would you like a drink?"

She accepted it, sniffing what smelled like vodka and cranberry juice. "Is this a Cosmo?"

"If you prefer something else, I will try to make it."

She gripped the glass tightly, wondering if it was coincidence he'd made her favorite drink, or if he'd been stalking her. "This is fine, thank you."

He gestured with one hand toward the table. "This way."

She let him pull her chair out for her and sat. He moved to the chair at the other end of the table. "Do you enjoy looking at the stars, or would you prefer another view?"

"I didn't realize the view could be changed." She'd been avoiding looking at the enormous screen in her bedroom because the vast open space made her dizzy.

He said, "Something more grounded, perhaps." Suddenly, the view changed to large trees dappled in soothing blue and magenta leaves. "The forest of Kirenai Prime."

She'd learned the name of Iroth's species from Zhinko, but hadn't seen images of their home planet. Anything she could learn about Kirenai might help her convince Iroth to let her go. She smiled. "That's beautiful."

Zhinko arrived carrying what looked like a platter balanced across two thin metal arms protruding from its egg-like body. "I thought you might enjoy freshly baked tartlets and a selection of roasted and glazed vegetables. All suitable for humans."

A third arm rose from a panel at the top of the egg and placed three tiny tarts on her plate along with some green, yellow, and orange bits covered in shiny golden sauce. Then the AI glided over and did the same for Iroth.

Realizing she was famished, Maise picked up a tartlet and nibbled one edge. The filling tasted savory and delicious, so she quickly devoured the entire thing. She'd never been a fan of vegetables, but they smelled good, so she ate them, too.

"Did Zhinko not offer you food while I was recovering?" Iroth said from the other end of the table, eyebrows raised.

She froze, suddenly realizing she'd been scarfing like a hungry dog. Swallowing, she sat up straight and set her fork aside. "Yes, but I wasn't hungry then."

Zhinko whizzed over with another tray in hand, nearly dropping it on the floor as the unit came to a halt near her chair. "Oh, dear. I allowed you to go hungry. I have been a terrible host."

"No, Zhinko, you've been wonderful. I just didn't realize I was hungry until now."

"You are our first guest on this ship, and I fear I may be out of practice with my hospitality programming." One of Zhinko's arms whisked her dish away while another arm placed a new plate loaded with what looked like a steak and purple mashed potatoes in front of her. "Please enjoy the main course tonight—*ijin'en* tenderloin and whipped *fahwe* root with herbed butter sauce."

Her mouth watered at the savory smell. "Did you actually cook all this, Zhinko?"

"I was originally programmed to perform hospitality on a G'naxian cruise liner. Unfortunately, the liner is no longer in business." The AI's tone dropped as if sad, and Maise wondered if alien computers had feelings. She'd have to be careful how she spoke to it from now on, just in case.

"Be sure to save room for dessert," Zhinko continued, more brightly this time. "I made *goviberry* pie and ice cream."

"Masterful as always," said Iroth, lifting his fork. "Thank you Zhinko."

Maise watched the AI leave. She hadn't been provided with a knife, but the steak was tender enough to cut with the edge of her fork. Taking a small bite, she nearly moaned out loud at the buttery succulence. Whatever *ijin'en* was, it was delicious.

Iroth sipped his Cosmo, his turquoise eyes following her every move. "How do you like your room?"

Her stomach turned, and she set her fork aside. It would be easy to get comfortable here if she allowed it. "It isn't my room."

He lowered his gaze to his plate. Was he ashamed? He seemed determined to keep her prisoner, yet he also seemed to want to please her.

She rose and approached his side of the table, taking a seat next to him. "Why won't you let me go home, Iroth? I won't tell anyone about you, I promise. I helped you back on Earth. Didn't ask too many questions. Took you at your word. Can't you take me at mine?"

He eyed his glass. "I don't think you understand what's at stake. The prince is looking for an assassin, and I'm the obvious culprit."

It was as if a lightbulb went off in her head. "My friend Georgie knows the prince! She was on his ship last I heard. And my friend Lora is working with his security person. Once I talk to them, I bet we can get the prince to listen to your side of the story."

"Stop." He spoke sharply enough to make her shrink back in her chair.

She gulped, just now realizing that any connection she might have to prince might make Iroth more wary of her, not less. "I—"

"I'm the bad guy and always will be. No one will ever give me the benefit of the doubt, no matter who you speak with."

She could feel her jaw trembling and the prickle of tears behind her eyes. The thought of never going home, never seeing her parents again, never finishing school or laughing with Lora and Georgie made her want to cry. But giving up wasn't something she was good at, otherwise she'd have quit vet school years ago.

Reaching over, she touched the back of Iroth's hand with her fingertips. "I haven't known you very long, but you don't seem like you want to be bad. I understand you think I'm a liability if you let me go. But will you please at least let me call my mom? She's sick, and I'm worried about how she'll do without me. You can listen in and stop me if I say anything you don't want. I'm begging you."

It was a long shot, and she was certain he was about to say no. But then he stood. He set his napkin aside and stood next to her chair. "Kiss me, and I'll let you make a brief call."

She sucked in a breath. "K-kiss you?"

He raised an eyebrow, a mischievous glint in his eye, as if he was daring her.

"You don't think I will, do you?" She pushed her chair back and stood on unsteady legs. Although he was holding her against her will, she didn't think he was a monster. He was just scared and trying to survive. If a kiss would allow her to call her mom, what was the harm?

Swallowing, she nodded. "One kiss."

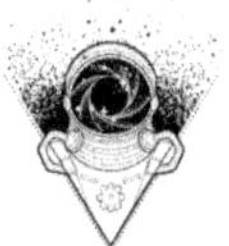

Using Maise's request to call her mom as leverage for a kiss was low; even a rogue like Iroth knew that. He'd expected her to reject him. To barter. And definitely he expected her to emanate disgust.

But as she rose to face him, he felt no disgust coming from her. In fact, he felt anticipation that matched his own. He could barely breathe. Allowing her to have contact with her family was probably a mistake, but there was something about Maise that made him want to please her, to help ease her sadness, no matter how irrational and careless that made him. He yearned to crush her against him, clamp his lips over hers, taste her sweetness and feel her warmth.

But he didn't. He remained perfectly still. Taking a kiss was not the same as being given one. She had to come to him, not the other way around.

She locked gazes with him for what felt like an eternity, as if waiting for him to move. His Iki'i felt her growing nervousness. It was as delicious as her arousal had been earlier.

Slowly, she put both hands on his shoulders and lifted onto her toes so she could reach his mouth. Her lips brushed his. A feathery touch, barely more than a breath.

His control fled.

He wrapped his arms around her waist and pulled her against him, leaning into her kiss and sweeping his tongue across her lips.

She gasped, going momentarily stiff. But her nipples hardened against his chest. Her fingers curled behind his neck and the tension fled her body as she molded herself against him.

He slid one palm up her spine to the base of her skull, tilting her closer. She tasted slightly of berries, and he probed his tongue into her mouth with broad strokes. She responded by opening wider and rolling her tongue around his as he thrust.

Oritzu, she was delicious, intoxicating. Irresistible. He let his other hand glide downward to cup her nicely rounded ass, grinding his insistent erection between their bodies. He'd been with women before, but never experienced any feeling except release. Maise made him want more than just release. So much more. He yearned for connection. For sanctuary. A safe place to rest. He'd give anything to feel her heat clamped around his cock, to drive into her until she cried out in ecstasy.

But then she broke the kiss. In a breathless voice, she said, "Okay, I kissed you."

His entire body was rigid with desire. He wasn't certain he had the strength to stop. *You've been reprobate enough for one evening,* he chastised himself. She'd fulfilled his request. If he took more now, that would be the end of any growing attraction she might have for him. They were going to be shipmates for a long time, and he didn't want her to hate him.

Dropping his hold, he stepped backward. "One kiss. One call."

She licked her lips and looked down to straighten her sweater. He could see the sharp points of her nipples even through the plush knit, and it made his cock throb harder. They were going to be together on this ship for a long, long time. If he didn't control his urges, he would eventually end up doing something stupid. *Like agree to let her make a call?*

He picked up his drink and took a long swig, the reality of what he'd promised now slipping over him like a shroud. But a deal was a deal.

Hoping he wasn't about to make the biggest mistake of his life, he said, "Zhinko, make a connection to Earth's cellular satellite system and place a call to Maise's mother. Audio only."

A few moments later, Zhinko said, "Ready, Captain."

A trilling sound repeated itself three times before a woman answered. "Hello?"

"Hi, Mom, it's Maise." Maise's voice was higher than usual, and he narrowed his eyes, ready to sever the connection if she so much as hinted at betraying him.

"Oh, hello, darling," the other woman said, her voice an older version of Maise's. "Did you want to come over for dinner? Your sister's here."

Maise's eyes looked glassy as she sank into her chair again. "Thanks, Mom, but I can't. I, um, I'm going to be out of town for a while. I wanted to let you and Dad know."

"Out of town? What about school?"

Other voices in the background sounded curious, and there was some shuffling before a male voice said, "Where're you going, Maise?"

"I… got a last-minute offer for a work-study program abroad. I'm going to be in and out of communication." She glanced toward Iroth.

He knew she was hoping for future opportunities to call, and licked his lips, unable to stop thinking about what she'd traded him for this one.

She flushed and dragged her gaze from his. But his Iki'i felt her desire.

"That sounds interesting," said another female he assumed must be Maise's sister. "Where will you be studying?"

Maise cleared her throat. "Lots of places. Mostly off grid. I hope to get to work with some exotic animals."

"How long will you be gone?" asked her mother. "What about the clinic?"

Frustration circled Maise like a dust devil and she rubbed a hand over her face. "My business manager has it handled, don't worry."

Her father said, "Come over for a goodbye dinner before you go. I'll grill burgers."

"I can't." The strain was coming through in Maise's voice. "I'm already en route. I had to jump, or I'd miss out."

"Oh, that is last minute!" Her father chuckled. "I hope this helps satisfy your travel bug."

The family talked a little more about Maise's imaginary trip, and Iroth had to give her credit; she was a good storyteller. Her parents seemed happy about her success. By the time the conversation ended, Maise was fighting tears, and he was swallowing guilt.

"Okay, I love you guys," she said.

"We love you too," said her father.

"Call again as soon as you can. We can't wait to hear all about it," her mother added.

The moment she hung up, a sob broke from her. "They're going to be heartbroken when I never come back."

Iroth gritted his teeth. He'd left his own family without a word, and the few times he'd checked on them, they were doing just fine without him. It'd been a mistake to open this wound for her. She'd be better off never contacting them again. Never being reminded of what she'd left behind. "They have another child to nurture. You'll be surprised at how quickly they'll get over your loss."

She lifted her splotchy, tear-stained face and scowled. "You're a bastard, you know that?"

Shoving her chair back, she rose and rushed toward the door with Bixby at her heels.

Zhinko entered as she was leaving. "Don't go yet. I've brought dessert!"

But she disappeared without a word, leaving the dining room hollow.

"She doesn't need dessert," said Iroth, tipping back the rest of Maise's Cosmo and stalking to the bar to pour himself something stiffer. He knew from experience she'd find little joy in anything for a good long while.

*M*aise paced the bedroom floor, tears she refused to let fall burning behind her eyes. *They'll get over your loss.* "What an asshole." She looked at Bixby where the dog stood near the door, watching her pace. "I can't believe he said that."

Maybe he was a monster, no matter how much she wanted to deny it. No matter how good he kissed, or how much he catered to her and Bixby's needs. He was keeping her against her will. And now her parents weren't even looking for her. Why had she bothered to make up such a plausible story? They were thrilled she was finally getting to travel. If they only knew the half of it.

She looked at the window over her bed, taking in the thick spray of stars across the blackness. Was she to be stuck on this ship for the rest of her life?

"Gah!" Picking up a glittering green figurine, she threw it across the room as hard as she could. It left a gash in the purple wall. "See how fast you get over that, Iroth." She got the sense he valued his ship more than anything.

Except right before her eyes, the damaged wall knitted itself back together as if it'd never happened. She stalked over and picked up the figurine. It was fine, too, made of emerald or some equally unbreakable stone.

"Argh!" She dropped it and flopped backwards across the bed.

Bixby hopped up beside her and laid her head on Maise's stomach.

She rubbed the dog's soft ears and imagined her parents and sister sitting around the dinner table, talking about the adventures she must be having. How long before they started to worry and called the police to start looking? Not that any Earth authorities could do much since she'd been abducted to outer space. And she imagined even alien space police might have a hard time finding a single ship among the millions of stars.

Over the next two days, she spent her time dozing or reading, expecting Iroth to show up at her door any minute. But he stayed away. Zhinko, however, was at her beck and call. The AI brought food and drinks, taught her how to play alien board games, and even turned out to be a decent conversationalist. She learned a lot about Kirenai, Fogarians, and the many other sentient species populating so many fascinating planets. *Well, you wanted to travel.* Would she ever actually get to walk on one of these exotic worlds?

But by the third day, she grew tired of being cooped up. Bixby was even more antsy. Maise stared at the closed door, contemplating leaving, even if only for a walk around the hallways. Except she dreaded running into Iroth. "You can't avoid him forever," she muttered to herself.

Before she could step forward, a knock sounded at her door.

Her heart leapt to her throat. Zhinko didn't bother knocking, which meant it could only be…

Iroth's muffled voice said, "If you're done being angry, I would like to show you the holo suite."

Maise crossed her arms, then sighed and stepped forward. The door opened. Iroth stood there wearing a checkered maroon button-down shirt under a black leather vest. She glared at him. "I'll never stop being angry at you. What's a holo suite?"

He closed his eyes and nodded once, as if absorbing her heated emotions. "A place Bixby will be able to run."

Her crossed arms relaxed slightly. "That would be nice."

"Come, then." He walked down the hallway.

She hesitated only long enough to take a deep breath, then followed. He led her to the lift she'd discovered on her earlier forays of the ship. She stepped inside after him, keeping as far to the other side of the car as possible. Bixby kept to her knee, a fuzzy wall between them. His cologne permeated the small space, and she forced herself to keep looking straight ahead instead of at his broad shoulders and square jaw. Why did her hormones threaten to take over every time she was around him?

The doors slid open, and he stepped from the car ahead of her. He threaded them through a room full of odd-looking furniture and a big platform that could be an alien version of a billiard table. A door in the far wall opened for him automatically to reveal a massive room with curved walls and grid lines that gave her a moment of vertigo. "Come stand here," he said, pointing to a spot next to him. "What's Bixby's favorite terrain?"

Maise approached slowly, unsure why he asked. "An open field, I guess."

Suddenly, they were no longer in a room. They were outside on a flat plain. Minuscule mahogany-colored leaves blanketed the ground. Barely visible in the murky distance, what looked like sharp mountain peaks rose into the azure sky, and a huge red sun burned overhead.

"Oh, my." Maise gaped at the vast expanse. A hot wind gusted past, and far in the distance, a herd of running creatures disappeared behind a swale.

Bixby barked happily and took several steps in that direction, pausing to see if Maise wanted to follow.

Maise said, "This is incredible." She raised one hand and walked forward, trying to recall how many steps would take her back to the door. "How do you keep from bumping into the walls?"

"You will never encounter a wall. The program has a looping function and the floor is designed to slide so you can feel like you're walking forever. When you finish, simply say 'end program'."

The landscape disappeared.

She grinned, her previous anger evaporating under a glow of excitement. "What else can it do? A beach? I'd love to walk on a beach."

Glittering gold sand appeared under their feet, lapped by gentle turquoise waves. The smell of salt filled the air, and a tiny, bluish sun that was barely more than a star created a sort of twilight across the entire sky.

Even so, it was delightfully warm, making Maise want to roll up her pant legs and wade in the surf.

She bent and picked up a curled white shell the size of her thumbnail. "Holy crap, this feels real." She looked at Iroth. "What happens if I try to take it out of here?"

He smiled. "You can't. This is simply a sensory immersion program. Nothing's real. You can swim in the water, and when you leave, you'll be fully dry."

She laughed and stepped into the waves, soaking her tennis shoes in very real-feeling warm water. "Come on, Bixby." Bending, she peeled off her shoes and socks, wanting to feel the sand underfoot. "Let's run!"

The dog barked once and splashed into the water joyfully. Together, they took off down the beach. It felt so good to run, to breathe the warm salt air. She kept expecting to hit the wall, but Iroth was right. She ran and ran, Bixby zig-zagging up and down the beach ahead of her.

Iroth jogged up behind her, grinning and obviously pleased she was enjoying this. "You may come here any time you like. There are many worlds programmed in our database."

She stopped and pushed her hair away from her eyes, breathing hard. Sweat rolled down her sides beneath her sweatshirt. Recalling the photo of him with his parents, she asked, "Will you show me Fogaria?"

His smile faded. "Why do you want to go there?"

"I saw a picture of you and your parents there."

His mouth formed a thin line. "Where did you find this picture?"

"In the ship's database—"

"Zhinko, erase the photograph."

"Wait, what? No!" she grabbed his wrist.

"My past is dead." He said through clenched teeth, the cords of his neck like thick ropes. The anguish in his eyes made her heart ache. What had happened to make him so desperate to leave his past behind?

She gripped his wrist harder. "Why are you so determined to be rid of anything connecting you to your past? Tell me the truth, Iroth. Are you the assassin?"

"No." His nostrils flared as he looked down into her face.

"Then why are you so desperate to disappear?"

He pulled his arm from her grip and turned to look out over the waves. "When I parted ways with my parents, I took a job hauling freight in the slums of Sireta station." He picked up a small stone and tossed it into the ocean. "It was backbreaking work, and the pay was terrible, but I was young and desperate. Most of us working there were. Our overseer was like a father to us. He protected and sheltered us. Even when he discovered I was a *burendo*, he treated me with respect and swore that as long as I worked for him, he'd never reveal my secret. But one day his son got caught stealing from the deliveries." His upper lip curled into a sneer. "Next thing I knew, I was in a detainment cell serving time while his kid went free."

"That's terrible! He framed you?" Maise shook her head. "And what's a *burendo*?"

Iroth thrust out one hand. The teal blue skin faded to gold, then deep ochre up to where his bicep disappeared under his sleeve. "Most Kirenai can assume the shape of any species in the galaxy, but not color. I can do both. I'm a mutation. A freak."

"Why would changing color make you a freak?" She examined his arm in awe. "I'd say that's pretty damn cool."

"That's not how the galaxy sees us. *Burendos* are dangerous. Unpredictable. Inclined toward crime." His arm resumed its teal color and dropped it to his side.

She shook her head. "But that doesn't mean they're right. People say pit bulls and rottweilers are inherently aggressive, but they're strong and loyal and protective and a lot of wonderful things if they're taught how to use those qualities for good. Sure, they can be trained to be bad, but so can any dog."

His nostrils flared, and he released a loud breath. "Are you comparing me to a dog?"

She flushed, realizing that's exactly what she'd done, even after throwing a stink at the shuttle about not being his dog. "I'm just using an example of how DNA doesn't define who we are on the inside. I mean, look at Bixby. Shelties aren't known for being interested in anyone but their owners, but she makes friends with everyone she meets."

He raised an eyebrow. "You just did it again."

She threw up her hands, the heat in her face intensifying. "I'm sorry, but dogs are what I know, all right?"

He grinned. "I forgive you. But if I make the mistake of using one of your dog signals again, you're not allowed to get mad."

She pursed her lips, trying not to grin back. "I can if you're being a jerk."

"Agreed." His smile turned lazy, and he tucked a loose curl behind her ear.

Suddenly, the way their gazes were connected felt alive with sparks, and Maise's breath caught in her throat. He stood close enough to kiss her if he wanted to. *Or for me to kiss him*. Except kissing him was the worst idea in the world, even if she wasn't all gross and sweaty under her shirt from her run on the beach.

She stepped back and looked for her dog. "Hiding like you are makes it look like you're guilty. You should stand up for yourself. I'll vouch for you if you let me go home."

He let out a heavy sigh. "It would do no good. The galaxy only views me with fear. I can't risk being tied to the massacre. Which means I can't let you go home. I'm sorry."

Bitterness resumed its place in her heart, but at least she understood where his fears were coming from. She patted her thigh and Bixby trotted over. "Come on, girl, time to go. End program."

The holo suite paradise winked out of existence. As she left the room, she felt Iroth's gaze at her back like a drowning man crying for help. But she couldn't help someone who wasn't willing to help themselves.

13

After Maise had gone, Iroth stood alone in the barren, gridded room, heart aching. Innocent or not, he was a monster. A deviant. A creature shunned by all who met him.

Maise doesn't think so.

She wanted him to stand up for himself. Had even offered to vouch for him.

He shook his head fiercely, clearing it of vacillation. He'd been lied to before. Coming forward would only result in his death. No matter who spoke on his behalf, the prince would never believe him, let alone the rest of the galaxy. Nobody believed a *burendo*, let alone one who'd been at the scene of the crime.

Yet a softness for this human female had crept into his resolve. He set the ship's systems to Earth's rotational cycle, and over the next days, he watched the news with her, hoping beyond hope someone caught the assassin. If the culprit was caught, he'd breathe a little easier. Perhaps even return Maise to her family, though his entire being balked at that idea for all the wrong reasons. He couldn't seem to get enough of her.

As time passed, she sat closer. Touched him more often. Even laughed at his stories when they weren't dark. He was surprised by the number of fond memories he could recall, encouraged by her sweet smile and addictive laughter. He adored her laugh. Lived for the brightness in her eyes. And his Iki'i sensed a growing affection he yearned to make permanent.

They spent many days in the holo suite, exploring different worlds. He discovered she enjoyed learning about cultures and art, and showed her the artifacts decorating his room, explaining how he'd discovered them. She shared her love of animals by showing him documentaries from Earth. In turn, he opened up the galaxy to her by showing her the galactic web, full of more information than she could ever consume.

When news of a royal wedding reached them, they sat next to each other on a plush sofa to watch her friend make her first public appearance on the arm of Prince Arazhi himself. Maise had her legs crossed on the cushions, her knee touching Iroth's thigh. Every time she touched him, all he could think about was pulling her even closer. He watched her while she watched the screen, her eyes glittering with excitement.

She covered her mouth with both hands. "Oh, my God. I can't believe Georgie's marrying a prince." Maise leaned forward and pointed to another woman with auburn hair in the background. "Look, there's Lora, too!" She sighed. "I wish I could be there."

Although she didn't say it as a request, he felt the tug on his resolve just the same. He wanted to give her everything.

"Would you like to call your family again?" he asked.

She turned to him, eyes wide. "Really?"

He nodded. "Just be careful what you say."

After the wedding ended, he turned off the screen and had Zhinko place the call. "Audio only, please."

On the first ring, her father answered. "Maise? Thank heaven you called. I'm in the hospital with your mom. She fell and hit her head." His voice hitched. "The doctors say it doesn't look good."

A wave of terror and grief slammed into Iroth's heart, and Maise's face turned ashen.

Bixby whined and licked the back of her white knuckles gripping the edge of her seat.

"Is Alison there?" she asked.

"Yes. Can you make it back? It might be…" her father's voice cracked again, "the last chance you get to see your mom."

Maise glanced at Iroth before burying her face in Bixby's ruff. Sobbing, she said, "I don't think so, Dad. Will you hold the phone to her ear?"

Iroth felt like he was encased in ice as she sputtered words of love and regret. His Iki'i resonated with her pleas for forgiveness, her gratitude, her grief.

And at that moment, Iroth knew. He knew everything he'd done was wrong. He'd been cruel and evil and self-serving. Maise had saved him. Even now, she continued to be faithful to her promises. She was good and kind and didn't deserve to suffer just to keep him safe, any more than he deserved to be blamed for crimes he hadn't committed. A fresh realization spiked through him with a solidity he'd never expected. *I love her.* He'd kissed her but once, had never enjoyed the pleasures of her body, yet he loved her. Maise was his mate, he was sure of it. And he was going to do what he could to make her happy, no matter the cost.

The moment she told her father goodbye, he said, "I'm taking you back to Earth."

She sucked in a breath and looked up, eyes red with tears. "What?"

"I'm taking you home. You should be with your family."

Her face crumpled, and fresh tears spilled from her eyes. "Thank you, Iroth." She threw herself into his arms. "Oh, thank you. You won't regret it. I'll never tell a soul about you. I swear to God."

He held her tight, breathing against her hair as she cried, his Iki'i warmed by relief and gratitude. Was this what it felt like to be a hero? It was likely the closest he'd ever get. His own heart was breaking, both at her pain and at the realization he'd no longer have her around to talk to. But it was the right thing to do.

Maise could hardly believe that after all this time, he was letting her go. She only wished it hadn't taken her mom's accident to convince him. But he apologized again and again as she clutched his chest, letting her sob, stroking her hair as they sat on the couch where they'd spent so much time together over the past few weeks.

He commanded Zhinko to turn the ship toward Earth, and she let a last shuddering breath ease from her chest. She felt so wrung out. And his arms were a comfort. His scent, familiar and warm.

She tilted her face to meet his gaze. The concern softening his eyes made her heart melt. Needing more comfort and unable to resist, she traced her lips across his mouth.

He smiled softly and closed his eyes. He'd never asked for another kiss after that first exchange. She might've thought he hadn't enjoyed it, except every look he gave her was full of desire. Desire he never acted on. Desire she never responded to. Even now, she could feel the bulge at his crotch nudging her hip while they hugged. *This could be your last chance.*

What she was thinking was probably a bad idea, but the comfort of a man's arms sounded like exactly what she needed right now. Swallowing nervously, she kissed him again, more firmly.

It was like a spark on gasoline. His posture shifted, the mood in the room suddenly heating.

She cracked her eyelids to find his eyes blazing with passion. She put her fingertips to his cheek. "Kiss me, Iroth."

Without hesitation, he dipped his head and claimed her lips like a thirsty man at a well. Her lips parted with a moan, and he slipped his tongue inside. They sparred, tongues tangling, lips twisting together. His hands spread across her back, pulling her tighter against him as if he never intended to let her go.

Gasping for breath, she broke the kiss, but only long enough to readjust herself so she straddled his lap. She needed to lose herself in this comfort and to find relief from her worry about her mother's accident. His muscles were hard, his thighs like granite boulders under her legs, and the lump at his fly pressed and throbbed against her jeans-covered center.

He planted a frenzied line of kisses along her jaw and down the curve of her throat.

She curled her fingers around his neck, tilting her head to one side and offering herself to him. Clawing at the back of his shirt, she raked it up over his head.

He shrugged free of it, then reached for hers, tearing it free before moving quickly to her sports bra to do the same. Her nipples puckered in the air, and he reached for her breast, hand cupping the mounded flesh as he bent his head to suck.

Rockets of sensation exploded through her and she arched her back, fingers in his hair as he nipped and sucked first one nipple, then the other. "Yes," she gasped.

He flicked open the button to her fly, then his large hot fingers slipped down the front, sliding to the top of her slit where her clit was already throbbing with need. With slow, gentle pressure, he circled, inching deeper and deeper into her folds. She widened her legs, but it wasn't enough. She wanted more. Needed all of him.

Standing, she shucked out of her jeans and panties at the same time, pushing them down around her ankles and stepping free. Standing naked before him, she looked up to find him sitting back, sucking on his finger, turquoise eyes blazing with desire. His bare chest flexed as he slowly rose from the couch and put a hand to the button of his jeans.

"Is this what you want, *itoshi?*" he asked, his voice a deep, throaty growl that made her pussy tremble.

Wetness flooded between her thighs. "Yes."

With a quick twist of his hand, his fly was open. His cock sprang free, massive and gorgeous, deep blue with a shiny bulbous head and a deep slit at the top already leaking white pearly liquid. His jeans slithered to the floor as if made of silk, and he stepped forward, pulling her against him, roughly claiming her mouth once more in deep, compelling strokes.

He tasted as good as he smelled, fresh and woodsy, and their naked skin pressed together ignited her body in places she hadn't known existed until this moment.

Clamping one arm around her waist, he lifted her feet off the floor and pivoted to lay her on the couch. He looked into her eyes for only a moment before he began worshipping her body with his mouth. He licked and kissed down her throat, along her collarbone, over her breasts and belly. When he reached her sex, he inhaled deeply and buried his face there, tongue snaking between her folds while his hands roved her legs, drawing her knees up around him. He kissed her inner thighs, running the rough edge of his jaw against the tender skin, then returned to her center, his fingers parting her lower lips as he delved deeper with his tongue.

She gasped and arched into him, her hips moving in a steady rhythm that matched his probing. He sucked her clit, and a thick finger entered her. Her vision flooded with a sea of stars as a sudden climax overwhelmed her and she exploded with pleasure. After stroking a few more times as her micro-shocks subsided, he climbed up her body and kissed her throat.

She panted, hands kneading his thickly muscled shoulders. He was driving her crazy with need, turning every square inch of her into an erogenous zone. Even her toes tingled as she ran the soles of her feet along the backs of his muscled calves.

His cock pulsed at the crease of her thigh, and she reached down, needing to feel him. Her fingers circled his girth, the velvet skin hot under her touch. He groaned and shifted his hips, thrusting against her.

"I want you," she gasped, angling the head of his shaft toward her entrance.

He pulled back, claiming her mouth as she centered him against her opening. In short, stuttering thrusts, he entered her, his tongue mimicking the thrusting as he stretched her, filled her, his heated length finally seating itself fully inside her with satisfying pressure.

"Maise," he murmured against her lips, continuing to worship her mouth while his hips pinned her against the cushions.

She bucked and squirmed, wanting—needing—him to move inside her. Needing to feel his long stroking thrusts entering her again and again.

He pulled back, plunged forward again, his rhythm increasing until he was pounding into her, his pubic bone meeting her clit every time he filled her.

The pressure building inside her was massive, an unbreakable thing. Her entire body trembled with the need for release. But every time she thought she might reach the cliff, he shifted his position, his rhythm, somehow taking her even higher.

She clawed at his back, cried out his name, thrashed her head from side to side, sure she couldn't take anymore. Then he rolled his hips, drove deeper than she thought possible, and she crashed over the edge.

A growl rose from him, and she felt something prod her ass as she shuddered. Then it was gone, and he was grunting as jets of heat filled her. She opened her eyes only long enough to see him staring down at her face, teeth clenched and lips pulled back as he came inside her, pulsing, pulsing. It was enough to send her into another wave of pleasure.

When they both could finally breathe again, he wrapped her in his arms and curled onto the couch behind her. She'd never felt this cared for, this cherished. But her contentment was bittersweet. This would soon be nothing but a memory.

She was going home.

14

Troth stood on the bridge with Maise beside him, her small fingers interlaced with his. Earth's transportation web was still disabled, and traffic to the surface was forbidden by royal edict. Two royal military cruisers patrolled in high orbit for unauthorized shuttles attempting to land. But the rest of the solar system was no longer off limits to travel, and commercial sightseeing cruisers and personal recreation vessels hovered in Earth's orbit like carrion birds.

He and Maise had spent the two days of travel to reach Earth enjoying each other's bodies. With each coupling, his desire to bond with her had grown, but he was proud he'd resisted. He was sending her home. Alone. He wouldn't secure the bond. He was a *burendo*, and mating him would only bring her shame. She should be free to pursue happiness without him.

A spiny gray G'naxian cruiser slid across the view screen, and Maise shook her head. "Why are there so many spaceships here?"

"They're curious. Earth is on the verge of being opened to travel, and they all want to see what has been hidden for so long. The emperor is wise to restrict travel, or they would flood your planet with visitors." *And probably black market traders.* His gut clenched at the thought of Maise being abducted and sold as a breeder. The emperor would try to stop the illegal trading, but undoubtedly some would slip through. "Be very cautious if you ever speak to an alien again."

She smirked and gave him a sideways glance. "Worried about me being abducted?"

"Yes." He met her gaze with as much seriousness as he could muster.

Her playful aura subsided, and she nodded. "Believe me, I won't fall for the wounded alien thing ever again."

"Good." He turned to where Zhinko hovered near the door. "Do we have enough cloaking crystals to get her home undetected?"

He'd transmitted a forged vessel signature to mask his ship's identity so he could mingle with the other spacecraft; they had to be in shuttle range if he hoped to get Maise home. But moving a shuttle to the surface without being detected would be a challenge, even with the cloaking technology. The military cruisers had advanced sensors, and he'd need to time her departure just right to avoid detection.

"I have scavenged the remaining crystals from the main ship's cloaking device," said Zhinko. "We have the capacity to fly the shuttle down and back."

"Getting her home is the priority," Iroth said. "If we end up leaving it behind, that's a sacrifice I'm willing to make."

A shard of Maise's fear pierced his Iki'i. "Are you sure I won't be shot out of the sky?"

He turned and took her shoulders so he could look into her eyes. "I wouldn't risk it if I thought there was a chance that would happen."

She took a deep breath. "Thank you." Wrapping her arms around his waist, she laid her cheek on his chest. "This means everything to me."

He hugged her tightly, resting his chin against the top of her head, breathing in her scent. He would never again smell *amai* wood incense without thinking of her. "I would do anything for you, *itoshi*."

He led her to the cargo bay where the shuttle waited.

At the base of the ramp, she paused. "Will I see you again?"

Sighing, he shook his head. There would be no more dishonesty between them. "No."

Indecision and regret tasted bitter against his Iki'i. She put her fingers over her lips a moment, pinching them as if doubting what she should say. Then she dropped her hand and took both his. "I enjoyed our time together, Iroth. Even if things started off on the wrong foot, you opened a galaxy of possibilities for me, and I'll cherish the time I spent with you."

The unfamiliar sensation of tears prickled behind his eyes. He held himself stiffly as he answered, "Your kindness was my undoing. I will never be the same, *itoshi*."

Her eyebrows pinched, and she tilted her head. "You've called me that several times now. *Itoshi.* What does it mean?"

He pressed her hands to his mouth. "Beloved one."

A small sound escaped her throat, and her green eyes filled with tears. "You love me?"

There was no sense in denying it. He nodded curtly. "Wherever you go, whatever you do, please take care of my heart."

She dropped her gaze, and doubt flooded his Iki'i. But it no longer bothered him. What she felt didn't matter. He loved her and would do anything for her. He nudged her toward the ramp. "Go on now. Your mother is waiting."

Without warning, she wrapped both arms around his neck and pulled him down to meet her mouth. This kiss was softer than the passion they'd shared over the last few days, yet just as urgent. He shared her breath, memorizing every play of her lips against his, the way her hands felt on his shoulders and neck, how she leaned into him, curves against planes.

When they finally parted, she said, "If you ever get a chance to come to Earth again, find me, okay?"

He knew he wouldn't be back. He hadn't committed the crime, but he could never return to the scene of it. Still, he nodded. "I promise."

Smiling, she stepped onto the shuttle and sat in the jump seat. Bixby nudged Iroth's hand, as though asking if he intended to come along. Iroth scratched behind the canine's ears and then urged her toward the ramp. "Not this time, Bixby. Take good care of her for me."

Bixby looked toward Maise, then back at him before slowly turning to join Maise on the shuttle. As the door closed and the ramp retracted, he felt like his heart was shriveling inside his chest, a heavy, useless weight he would never use again.

Turning, he left the cargo bay and everything that mattered behind.

Engulfed in the awkward beanbag jump seat again, Maise watched the ground loom closer until the shuttle settled into the clearing near the pulp mill. *Right back where I started.* Only she was no longer the same person who'd left Earth. Her chest felt tight, but how much of that was from the flight and how much was from her regret about leaving Iroth, she couldn't tell.

The jump seat released her with a whoosh, and Zhinko's voice filled the cabin. "Welcome back to Earth, Maise."

She struggled out of the seat. "Thank you, Zhinko, and good luck. I hope I get to talk to you again some day."

"Likewise, Maise. You and Bixby were a delight to have on board."

Bixby was already halfway down the ramp, apparently eager to get home.

Maise hurried after her. As expected, her Jeep was no longer in the pulp mill's parking lot, and she had to walk back to her apartment. About a half an hour later, she stood outside Yappy Hour. The brick-walled building seemed smaller than she remembered, more like a prison than a kennel. The stairway up to her apartment thudded hollowly under her feet as she went to retrieve her phone. Luckily, it was still there, plugged in next to her bed as if she'd only been gone a day.

But the apartment smelled disgusting, with a rank odor coming from her fridge. She didn't dare open it That was something for future Maise to take on, after she'd seen her mom.

She dropped Bixby off at the kennel downstairs, called an Uber, and within a few minutes was headed to the hospital. Her dad and sister were sitting outside the ICU.

"Maise!" they both cried together, sweeping her into a group hug.

She gripped them back fiercely, emotions too raw to speak.

Her father cupped her cheek and pressed a kiss to her forehead. "I'm so glad you could make it back."

"Me too, Dad," she choked out. He looked rumpled and tired, his gray polo shirt stained by what looked like mustard, and a haze of gray stubble sprinkled across his chin. "Can I see her?"

"The nurse should be finished by now." He led the way to a small room where Mom lay as if sleeping, a tube beneath her nose and IV lines running to her arms. Her head was bandaged, but a big purple bruise peeked from the edge near one temple.

Throat tight, Maise took her mom's hand, noting how papery and light it felt. Tears blurred her vision. "Hi, Mom. It's me, Maise. I'm here."

The slow, steady beeps from the monitors were all that answered.

"Sorry I was gone so long." The words would barely leave Maise's throat. "But I'm here now. I've seen so much, done so much. I can't even begin to describe…" she tapered off, knowing her father and sister were listening. Instead, she pressed her lips to the back of her mother's frail hand.

The small room was crowded with all of them there, but the nurses overlooked the two-person minimum and brought in an extra chair. The family sat with Mom well into the night, reminiscing about things with both laughter and tears.

Some time in the wee hours of the morning, when the conversation had subsided, and they were all in a half-doze, the monitors went static. A low beeeeeeep filled the room.

"No!" both Maise and Alison gasped. "Mom! Don't leave us. Please, mom."

The monitor continued to sing its mournful note.

Dad, stoic as ever, bent and kissed his wife's cheek.

Maise frantically went to the door, looking for a nurse, but her dad put a hand on her shoulder. "She didn't want to be resuscitated, remember?"

Tears choked Maise's eyes and throat. Mom had signed a living will years ago, before her dementia had taken over. But all Maise wanted was to once more see the strong and vibrant mother of her youth.

She and her sister held each other, sniffling, and watched the nurses come in, turn off the machines, and pull Mom's IV and oxygen tubing. Mom looked as if she was sleeping.

As soon as the nurses were gone, Maise lay her head against the mattress beside her mother's body and sobbed.

Eventually, a warm hand touched her shoulder, and her dad's voice said, "They need to take her now, Maise. Come on."

She left the hospital in a daze and went back to her parents' house. Everything looked the same, as if Mom might come back at any moment. A basket of half-finished crochet work near the recliner, ready for her to pick up where she left off. Family photos on every wall.

Dad went to bed, and Maise and Alison curled up on either side of him, holding hands across his chest.

When morning came, they went with him to the funeral parlor. He and Mom had made arrangements long ago, and after signing the papers, Maise took her dad to lunch at a sports bar close to Yappy Hour. Mom used to order takeout from here when she ran the clinic, and everything on the menu made Maise want to cry.

"I'm sorry I wasn't here, Dad."

He smiled at her. "Mom understood. You know she was thrilled for you, right? I know she gave you a lot of pressure about the business, but she was happy that you were following your dream."

That brought a fresh bout of tears and a shitload of guilt. If Mom only knew. But Maise couldn't say a word about what she'd really been doing, and Dad wouldn't understand if she did.

"Can you stay for the funeral?" he asked.

She swallowed and looked away. How was she supposed to tell him she wouldn't be going back to a dream veterinary sabbatical that had never existed?

He took her hand, concern creasing his face. "I hope you didn't burn any bridges to come back here. She'd want you to be happy, Maise. We both do."

Taking a shuddering breath, Maise shook her head. "It's too late to go back."

"Naw, that can't be." He squeezed her fingers. "Whoever's running things will understand, I'm sure. You just need to talk to them."

Numbly, she nodded. If only she could. She had no way to contact Iroth, and even if she did, he wouldn't be able to send the shuttle for her.

The shuttle. She sat up straighter. Iroth had said getting the shuttle back to the ship would be tricky. That he was willing to abandon it, but he planned on trying to find a window when the military ships weren't watching. If it hadn't left yet, she could try to call him. Or perhaps even return to his ship and surprise him. Would he want to travel the stars with her?

She stood so quickly her chair almost toppled. "I love you, Dad. Thank you."

"Of course, honey." He chuckled as she kissed his cheek. "Go on. I'll get the check."

She rushed back to Yappy Hour and grabbed Bixby.

Her assistant held his hands out in question. "Am I the only one who works around here?"

"You're in charge, Ted. Tell Monica I'm giving you a raise."

And with that, she was rushing back to the clearing and praying she made it in time.

15

*T*roth had lingered in orbit longer than he should, delaying the order to bring the shuttle back to the bay. He told himself he was waiting to be sure the military ships wouldn't spot it. But in reality, he just wasn't ready to leave. The taste of Maise's kiss on his lips was like a lifeline to another definition of himself, one he'd never believed could exist. Preparing to leave felt like preparing to cut off a limb.

He scrubbed his hands over his human face, wondering if he'd ever have the will to shift out of this body again. He liked how this form felt, the ease it gave him around Maise. Each muscle and plane had a memory for him now, her fingertips tracing here, her lips kissing there.

Then it occurred to him. Shape wasn't really the issue. What if he didn't try to look less human, but *more*? He stared at the glowing blue and white planet below, suddenly realizing how much of an idiot he'd been. He wanted a new identity. Creating one on Earth would be easy if he looked fully human. Galactic databases had not yet catalogued earth's individuals.

He could make a life with Maise.

He extended his teal-blue hand and focused on changing color. The skin faded, becoming pale, then blossoming golden brown similar to Maise's skin tone. *Easy.*

Excitement making his heart race, he asked, "Zhinko, how soon until the shuttle can return?"

"The shuttle just returned to the cargo bay, Captain. Maise is on board and wished to surprise you. But I fear we have another urgent matter. We have been boarded, Captain."

Feeling like he had whiplash, Iroth scowled. *Maise is back?* His ship was being invaded? "*Kuzara!* By whom? And how?"

"The invading shuttle is registered to Senbur Uragi Rhimono. They were cloaked and slipped inside when I opened the door for the shuttle. I have suggested Maise hide in the shuttle's smuggler's hold."

Iroth snatched a kinetic pistol from the locker on the bridge and ran toward the cargo hold. Uragi was the client who'd wanted a human female from the auction. *He probably wants the down payment back.* His blood turned cold. *Or he wants Maise.* He had to keep them from finding her. He reached the hatch to the cargo bay and skidded to a halt.

Three Kirenai and a pink scaled Qalqan stood on the docking bay floor beside a second, smaller shuttle, weapons drawn. And they were headed straight for Maise's shuttle.

"Hey!" Iroth shouted, stepping into the cargo bay. "The authorities are on the way, so I suggest you get the *kuzara* off my ship while you still can."

The Kirenai leader was in the shape of a Qalqan, as well, with a long, blue lizard snout, scales and a stubby tail. He leveled the muzzle of his gun at Iroth, lipless mouth gaping in a facsimile of a smile. "I seriously doubt you called the authorities, *burendo*."

Iroth gripped his pistol tighter and took a step closer. "I don't have your money, if that's what you're after. Go talk to the IDA."

"The money isn't my concern." Uragi waved a dismissive claw before placing it reverently over his chest. "I'm here to protect the empire." His voice dripped with sarcasm, and an identifying sensation that reminded him of ammonia reached Iroth's Iki'i.

Like a flash, the final moments at the auction swept through him; his gaze locking with a fellow Kirenai, the fleeting sense of ammonia, then the other Kirenai collapsing. Uragi had faked his own death?

Just like I did.

"You were at the auction," Iroth accused.

Uragi lifted his chin and chortled. "You're the only guest unaccounted for, *burendo*. The transportation web logs will verify it."

Iroth felt like he'd been frozen in ice. The contract had been a setup. Uragi hadn't wanted a human female—he'd wanted a scapegoat for the assassination. And Iroth had played right into his hands.

"You set me up," Iroth gritted between his teeth.

Uragi made a ticking noise and shook his head. "That's not how the emperor will see things. I'm about to be a hero." He pointed to a pair of Kirenai detention manacles in the Qalqan's hands. "Come now. You know you can't win in a gunfight."

Iroth's attention fell to Uragi's weapon. A laser pistol, not kinetic. The Kirenai guards behind him held matching weapons. Lasers were one of the few weapons deadly to Kirenai, and even a ship's self-healing *popotan* bulkheads could be irreparably destroyed by laser fire. Most captains banned such guns from even coming on board.

If it'd been only his own life at stake, Iroth would've fought claw and fang before surrendering. But he couldn't afford a laser fight on deck, not while Maise was in the shuttle. The best thing to do would be to get Uragi and his men off his ship as soon as possible.

Stepping forward, he let the manacles clamp over his wrists. Pain flared up his arms, followed by a wave of nausea. He frowned. He'd been manacled before and expected the familiar wash of chemicals that would temporarily prevent him from changing form. This was not that. Yet it was also familiar.

Uragi gestured toward the shuttle. "In there."

Maise. Iroth surged forward. "Just take me and go—"

A guard slammed a fist into his gut, doubling him over. Then a knee to his head made the deck spin out from under him. The nausea he'd felt from the manacles now turned to vertigo. His matrix shuddered. His vision narrowed to a pinpoint, then blackness.

I'm losing my form, he realized.

The last thing he remembered as he fell to the deck was the sound of a dog barking.

The shuttle thunked to the deck, and the jump seat released Maise before the floor stopped vibrating. She struggled to her feet. On the shuttle's screen, another shuttle smaller than the one she was in sat on the opposite side of the deck, this one shaped more like a bullet than a rosebud. A group of aliens were climbing out of it, three blue and one that was bright pink.

"Zhinko, what's happening?" she asked.

"I apologize for the discomfort, but I must ask you to hide in the smuggler's hold. The ship has been boarded." A panel popped open beside her jump seat.

Fear settled in her chest. "By who?"

"I believe it is Uragi Rhimono," said Zhinko. "The client we were supposed to deliver you to."

Shit. Was Iroth going to get in trouble for not fulfilling his contract? Maise pushed Bixby into the small space that had opened. "Can't we just give him his money back?"

"He does not appear to want money."

Maise gulped. If he didn't want money, that probably meant he wanted a female. *Me*. She tried to squeeze into the small space beside Bixby, but there wasn't room for both of them. Feeling panicked, she said, "There isn't room in here, Zhinko."

The row of jump seats separated, revealing a long crack at the base of the wall. "Then I suggest one of you hide in the engineering compartment."

"Bixby, lay down," she commanded.

The dog obeyed with her ears tucked back, sensing her owner's terror.

Maise hurried to the other compartment. She had to lie on her stomach to squeeze sideways into a coffin-sized area amidst the wiring and something squishy she didn't want to think about. Then the seats slid back into place, leaving her in darkness.

Heart beating loud in her ears, she tried not to gag at the sharp, oily smell surrounding her. What was happening to Iroth? Was he going to be all right?

The sound of booted feet thudded outside her hiding spot.

She held her breath, staring blindly into the darkness. *Please don't find us.*

A deep voice rumbled in a language she didn't understand, and someone started pounding on walls. She felt like she was about to suffocate.

Then Bixby began barking.

"No no no!" Maise whispered, hands clenching into fists near her head.

Bixby yipped and went silent.

Bixby? Maise gasped for air. What had they done? She needed to get out, but couldn't move in the small space.

The deep voice rumbled again and boots thudded away.

After a few minutes, the jump seats parted. Maise struggled out. Bixby's panel was still closed, and she rushed over, dreading what she might find inside. "Open it!"

The panel slid open, but the only thing inside was a scrap of gray fabric and some broken glass shoved into the back corner.

She spun, looking around the rest of the shuttle as her entire body trembled with adrenaline. "Where's Bixby?"

"I am sorry," Zhinko's voice sounded like a whisper. "They have taken her."

"Did they kill her?" Maise rushed from the shuttle.

"She appeared to be alive," said Zhinko.

The docking bay door was closed and the bullet-shaped shuttle was gone. "We need to go after them! Where's Iroth?"

Maise spun to look for him and spotted a gelatinous blue puddle. Her throat tightened. She'd seen this before. At the auction. She fell to her knees beside the puddle. "Iroth?"

The gel rose, as if trying to reach for her, then collapsed again. "Zhinko!" she screamed. "Zhinko, he's still alive! Do something."

She could barely breathe.

Zhinko whooshed in from the hallway, trailing what looked like a plastic tub. "Medical emergency protocols engaged. Please stand back."

Gulping back hopeless tears, Maise scrambled out of the way. It was Iroth. She knew it. This was happening because he'd brought her home. Uragi had come looking for her and probably taken Bixby as a consolation prize. And now Iroth…

Within moments, the AI had levitated the gel into the tub and rushed back through the halls and into the lift. Maise squeezed in beside them. The doors opened on the lower level, and Zhinko said, "The captain has forbidden guests on this level."

She pushed past and stepped off the lift. "Yeah, well, he's not here to stop me this time."

The AI didn't say more. It rushed them to a small room dominated by a large open coffin that looked as if it was made of stone. Zhinko emptied Iroth into it and, in a flurry of arms, began connecting tubes and pushing buttons.

She gripped the doorframe. "What's wrong with him?"

"It appears he is poisoned again. Beginning detoxification."

Why would Uragi poison Iroth instead of shoot him? It didn't make sense. "Will he be all right?"

The AI flashed with multicolored light. "I am uncertain. We used a significant portion of our medical supplies during the last purge process."

Maise swallowed, trying not to hyperventilate as she stared at the coffin. He couldn't die. She wouldn't let him. "If we need medicine, how do we get it?"

"The captain usually trades for supplies on Sireta station."

"How long will it take to get there?"

"Several of your Earth days, but I fear he will not survive that long."

Fighting panic, she thought of all the ships in orbit around them. "What about the ships nearby? One of them probably has what we need. We could call for help. And we need to get Bixby back."

Zhinko said, "The captain has ordered that you are not to have access to communications or other core ship systems."

She scowled. "Screw the captain's orders. This is an emergency."

"I'm afraid my programming will not allow me to disobey. We are to maintain our cover identity until I receive orders."

She stepped into the room and gripped the edge of the stone tub. "Iroth, if you can hear me, you have to give me control of the ship. You have to trust me."

The gel shuddered. Pulled together then parted with a sigh. "Yesss."

"You heard him, Zhinko." She glared at the egg-shaped robot. "He said yes."

"Acknowledged. Who would you like to call?"

She ached with relief, yet remained clenched with terror. Iroth was dying while she was arguing with a machine. "Just send a general request for the medicine."

"Please be advised that a general transmission will alert the royal military ships. They will be the first to arrive, and will undoubtedly place Iroth under arrest."

Her jaw trembled. *I'd rather see Iroth in jail than dead.* And if anyone was likely to have the right medicine, it was a military ship. "Do it. Tell them that Uragi stole my dog while you're at it. I want Bixby back."

"Right away, Maise."

"Iroth, you're going to be okay." She'd come back to the ship full of hope, full of dreams to follow, full of love for a big, blue-skinned alien with a chip on his shoulder. She had to save him. "I want to see the stars together. Hold on for me. Help is coming."

Troth fought for consciousness. Fought for life. He'd given control of his ship to the only person in the galaxy he trusted and now he was under arrest.

But he was alive.

He faded in and out of consciousness as unfamiliar healers looked into his resting pod. Medication burned through his matrix. The dizzying nausea of dialysis swept through him again and again.

All the while, all he could think was that his worst fears had come to pass. But he also knew Maise hadn't betrayed him on purpose. She'd come back to him. She'd done what she could to save him. If he died now, he'd die knowing his one true love didn't hate him. She was alive and well. And that was worth dying for.

His matrix tightened and separated, solidified and melted. Finally, after long agony and uncertainty, he cracked open his eyes. He'd resumed his human form, lying on a bed and staring up at a pale gray ceiling. The air felt like torture against his raw skin, and the soft white light in the room may as well have been a million suns blazing against his eyes.

He groaned and sucked in a breath. The fruity smell of regen fluid. A faint whiff of *amai* wood incense. A soft voice.

"Iroth?"

He turned his head to find a goddess's green eyes focused on him from a seat beside his bed.

She leaned forward. The love that bathed his Iki'i was as healing as any medicine.

"Maise?"

She smiled, and a cool hand touched his burning cheek. "Welcome back."

"Where am I?"

"The royal infirmary."

He blinked, trying to make sense of her words. "Prison?"

"No. The emperor's palace." Maise bent and kissed him, her relief against his Iki'i strong enough to make him swoon. She gently stroked the back of his hand. "You've been in and out of consciousness for days."

"What happened?" He didn't understand. He'd expected to be dead, or at the very least, in prison.

"Uragi tried to frame you." Holding his hand, she explained everything, her love never wavering.

The manacles hadn't been detainment manacles, they'd injected him with the poison used in the massacre. Then Uragi's men had planted a broken poison bottle on the shuttle as evidence. The only reason Uragi hadn't discovered her there was because they'd come across Bixby first. "The asshole took her captive as a cover-up for why he'd visited your ship. He tried to tell the authorities he'd bought her from you."

Apparently, Uragi had intended to wait long enough to let Iroth die from the poison, then alert the authorities that a *burendo's* ship was in orbit. With the planted evidence, everyone would assume Iroth was the assassin responsible for the massacre on Earth and that he'd been accidentally killed by his own toxin.

Except that Maise's quick call for help had saved his life. "Zhinko had video footage of Uragi's minion planting the evidence and abducting Bixby. After you were arrested, I had Zhinko call Lora and Georgie. We made sure you got a fair trial."

He took a moment to glance around the sterile room, his mind reeling. "Where's Bixby? Is she okay?"

Maise grinned. "She's fine. She's with Lora's dog, Pepper, in the gardens right now. I think she'll be a little more cautious about strangers from now on, though. She lost a tooth trying to bite the asshole who captured her."

He had to smile. *Good dog.* "And Uragi? Did they catch him?"

"He and his henchmen are locked up on a prison moon. I guess the emperor is planning a formal execution. There are still more collaborators on the loose, though. I guess the conspiracy runs pretty deep."

A male voice interrupted, "We still have some questions about that, if you don't mind."

Iroth turned his head and saw a blue human with long hair standing at the doorway: Zhiruto, the prince's bodyguard from the auction.

Maise smiled at him, affection obvious against Iroth's Iki'i. His heart threatened to crack. How long had he been unconscious? Had she transferred her affections so easily? *She's mine.* He sat up, breathing through the dizziness threatening to bowl him over.

"*Oritzu*, take it easy." Zhiruto stepped inside.

Behind him, another Kirenai waited in the hall, one who could only be Prince Arazhi, dressed in a black and yellow tunic and wearing a narrow crown on his head. Maise's human friend, Georgie, stood at his side, her blonde hair held back by a circlet of gold.

"Come in." Maise stood, making room for the newcomers. "Where's Lora?"

"She received information about another black market slave ship and went to manage the rescue team," said Zhiruto.

The prince stepped forward, gaze entirely on Iroth. "I understand you're a *burendo*."

Ah, here it is. The moment of truth. When Iroth's real fate was decided. He gripped the edge of his mattress and swung his feet off the edge. "I am."

"I'd like to offer you a job," the prince said.

Iroth frowned, confused enough that he momentarily considered lying back down. "Why?"

The prince cut a glance toward Maise. "I've been told you're trustworthy."

Maise was holding Georgie's hand and biting her lower lip. Had she arranged this?

He returned his full attention to the prince. "What kind of job?"

"My spy network could use a man like you. Someone who can truly blend in. The royal healer who tried to kill the emperor is still on the loose."

Iroth shook his head slowly. "I'm not really a palace guard sort of guy. More of a smuggling, thieving, espionage sort of guy."

The prince chuckled. "That's why you're perfect. No one will suspect you're on our side. But you're free to say no, of course."

Iroth took a deep breath. 'Free to say no' didn't always mean free to go. "And if I decline?"

"Then as soon as you're ready, you can leave. Your AI is waiting in orbit with your ship."

He looked again at Maise. All he cared about was her. And if she thought that a job with the prince would somehow make the galaxy accept him, she was wrong. He needed her to understand that. "Can I think it over?"

"Absolutely." The prince nodded. "I'm glad to see you've recovered."

Georgie kissed Maise on the cheek and whispered, "I'm glad he's okay."

Once everyone had gone, Maise sat beside him on the bed.

He adjusted his legs to face her. "What's going on? Do you want me to work for the prince?"

She shrugged. "I don't care who you work for, as long as you don't have to hide anymore."

He took her hands in his and looked at them, admiring her golden brown skin and finely shaped nails. His greatest desire was to bond with Maise. To give her the future she dreamed of. But she didn't understand what it would mean to bond with a *burendo*. "Even if I work for the prince, I'm still a monster. The prince will never trust me. The guards will never trust me." He swallowed thickly, hating what he was about to say. "If we're together, everyone will as shun you as they do me."

She squeezed his hands. "That's not true. The prince does trust you, or you wouldn't be here. We have my friends. And I'm a firm believer that the way to gain someone's trust is by trusting them first." She winked at him. "Just take you and me as an example."

He shook his head, still full of doubt. She had come back to him, even after what he'd done and despite what he was. If Maise wanted him to do this, he would try. He would do anything for her. Kill for her. Suffer for her. Die for her. She held his heart whether he willed it or not and was the one person in the universe who saw through what he was and into his soul. And she had faith in him.

Nodding, he said, "All right. I'll give it a try."

Georgie had tried to talk Maise into a big wedding on Earth, but small and intimate was more Maise's style. So they were holding the ceremony on board Iroth's ship with a handful of her family and friends. Iroth had managed to get the holo suite to look exactly like her parents' church, right down to the snag in the carpet at the door to the sanctuary.

Now she stood ready to walk down the aisle, her father next to her in his best Sunday suit. Bixby had just carried the ring pillow saddled to her back down the aisle, and it was time for Maise to go.

Dad held out his arm. "Ready?"

She glanced down at her simple, cream-colored gown and nodded. She'd tried on what felt like hundreds of wedding dresses before settling on the silky, off-shoulder wrap gown with a small, ruffled fold at the waistline that made it feel elegant without being gaudy. Gripping her bouquet of violet and cream roses in one hand, she took her father's arm with the other and started down the aisle.

As they passed the empty pew where she'd spent many childhood Sundays with her head in her mother's lap, her eyes pricked with tears. It wasn't really their church, but she knew her mom was here. That she'd approve, even if it didn't include becoming a vet.

Taking a deep breath, Maise turned from her past and focused toward her future.

Iroth stood waiting at the altar in a classic tuxedo, a small spray of red and purple *jargoth* feathers on his lapel. The feathers were Fogarian, the same ones that covered the statues in his room. She'd tried to get him to contact his family for the wedding, but he wasn't yet ready to reunite with them. Someday, she hoped, but he would do it in his own time. Meanwhile, he had her family, who already loved him to pieces.

She reached the altar, and he gave a deep bow to her father before accepting her hand. After several family meals together, Iroth and her dad had hit it off, arguing about classic spy movies. They'd ended up in the living room binge watching Alfred Hitchcock movies three nights in a row.

Zhinko hovered beside the groom with a boutonniere affixed to its black casing, proud to have the title "Best AI." At first, Lora had laughed at Iroth's choice of Best Man, but Maise pointed out that Zhinko was it. Iroth had lived in solitude and had no friends. But he was developing camaraderie with Zhiruto and Arazhi, who were serving as groomsmen to match Maise's bridesmaids: Alison as Maid of Honor, plus Georgie and Lora, all resplendent in their deep purple gowns.

"You look gorgeous," Iroth said in a low voice as she took her place beside him.

She beamed, glad they'd instructed the church pastor to make the ceremony short. When it was time for the vows, Iroth turned to her with the most serious expression she'd ever seen on his face. He took her hands and locked his gaze with hers. "Maise, I don't deserve you. Your kindness and optimism have changed my life forever. You've seen me at my worst, and love me even so. Thank you for taking a chance on me. Thank you for inviting me into your family. And most of all, thank you for teaching me to trust again. I'm honored to be your mate from now until the end of time."

Her throat felt tight as he placed a ring with a diamond the size of her thumbnail on her finger. Her dress might be simple, but Iroth had insisted on the ring after seeing a "diamonds are forever" commercial while watching Hitchcock.

She licked her lips and poised a gold and diamond ring that was almost as gaudy as hers over his finger. She wasn't as eloquent as he was, but every word she spoke came straight from her heart. "Iroth, I promise to love you forever and to trust you with my heart. I look forward to a lifetime of adventures together."

The pastor smiled and nodded. "Congratulations. I now pronounce you mates for life."

The music began once more, and they raced down the aisle together under a shower of holo suite rice. The church doors gave way immediately to a ballroom—unlike the real church back home. Zhinko had prepared food, and hours of drinking and dancing later, Maise was glad to collapse into bed next to her husband, still buzzed from champagne.

He stroked her curls away from her cheeks and kissed her nose. "My beautiful bride."

Happier than she'd ever imagined possible, she smiled as his hand curled around her ear and trailed down her throat with a feathery touch that made her giggle. "I think I drank too much."

His stroking stopped. "Would you like to wait?"

He'd insisted they shouldn't form the Kirenai mate-bond until the human ceremony was complete. She was pretty certain it was because he was giving her the option to change her mind right up until the last minute.

"Absolutely not," she said, putting his hand on her breast and making him pinch the nipple through her satin chemise.

He made a low, sexy noise and leaned in to kiss the curve of her throat.

A shiver rocked her. She slid her hand down his arm to his chest and lower, slipping inside his silk boxers to find his thick primary shaft already throbbing and ready.

They'd been intimate many times before the wedding, and she'd discovered he had a second cock just below his primary one. His mating shaft, he called it. Apparently, when he used it, it would share his DNA with her and form an unbreakable bond that would give her health and long life.

But right now she gripped his primary shaft firmly, feeling it pulse and swell beneath her palm. "God, I love this thing."

He flexed his hips, pumping against her, and nibbled his way up her throat to find her mouth. His tongue was firm and insistent, prodding her lips apart and delving into her mouth with seductive sweeps.

She loosened her hold on his cock and slid her hand around to find the smaller shaft below. It was stiff and shorter than his primary shaft, about the thickness of her thumb. He shuddered at her touch and pulled back. "Not so fast, *itoshi*. Let me prepare you."

He rolled her onto her back and cupped her breast with one hand, rolling and pinching the nipple while he kissed her again. She wriggled underneath him, dragging her chemise up over her head and tossing it aside. "I don't want any barriers."

He dipped down and sucked a nipple hard into her mouth, sending electric jolts straight to her pussy. His hands were like fire, blazing against her skin. He dragged a palm down her ribs and circled one hip, kneading her ass cheek as he moved down her body with small, biting kisses. She wore no panties, and he licked her right between the thighs before sucking gently on her clit.

She gasped, flexing her hips toward him. Spreading her knees farther apart, he brushed his tongue over the nub again and again, circling and teasing until she was panting, bucking up in time to his rhythm as her legs trembled and her nails dug into his shoulders.

Right as she was on the verge of orgasm, he thrust his tongue deep into her channel. She came, throbbing hard as his tongue stroked in and out.

He climbed back up her body, running his stubbled chin gently over her stomach. He sucked hard on a nipple, then moved to her throat, his erection prodding her slick folds. As he claimed her mouth, she rocked her hips, trying to take him inside. His tongue had been amazing, as always, but she needed all of him.

The head of his cock teased her opening as she writhed, satisfaction kept just out of reach. She growled against his mouth, "Stop it, you tease."

Chuckling, he penetrated her, quick and deep.

She gasped and flexed, taking every hot inch until his pubic bone crushed against her clit. He felt so good, she almost came again. Her ridges fluttered around him, and she pulled his mouth to hers to kiss him once more.

With a slow building rhythm, his hips began to move. He pumped in and out, pressing her into the mattress, body hot and heavy between her legs. He pushed into her harder and faster until she was panting his name, her juices slippery between their bodies.

She was near climax again when he reached around her backside, his fingers finding her slickness. He eased one digit against her ass as he continued to pump, more slowly now, deeper and deeper. Her impending orgasm doubled in size, tripled until she thought she might burst.

"Are you ready, *itoshi?*" his voice was a choked off growl.

"Yes, yes." She lifted her knees and spread her legs wide, opening herself to him.

He pulled back, and his finger left her ass. Then he sank forward again, both shafts penetrating her, filling her. They pulsed and swelled, a perfect unison of sensation as he drew back and entered her again.

Her eyelids fluttered. Moaning a long, loud cry, she shattered, her entire body clenching and releasing in a wave of pleasure so intense, the universe seemed to tilt. Her legs shook, her breath stopped, her heart pounded so hard and fast she thought it might burst.

She was vaguely aware of Iroth growling her name, a long deep note that resonated with her shuddering body. He continued pumping into her hard and fast, skin slapping skin until heat jetted from both his shafts. An aftershock rocked her, taking her almost as high as the first release.

He collapsed on top of her, breath heavy against her ear as they floated together for long minutes.

After their breathing eased and their skin cooled, he propped himself onto his elbows and looked into her face. His turquoise eyes were shining with love. "Are you ready to see the galaxy with me, *itoshi?*"

She snuggled against his chest. "Absolutely, my love. But can we get some sleep first?"

*D*ear Reader,

Thanks for reading! I had a ton of fun creating this unique, shapeshifting species, and hope you enjoyed them, too. Let me know if you did! Oh! And be sure to sign up for my VIP Club newsletter to get all the latest info about my releases, sales, exclusive giveaways, and cool stuff about me and my life in Alaska.

https://join.tamsinley.com/newsletter

If you haven't read my other books yet, check out my Galactic Pirate Brides series.

With no females of his kind left, Captain Qaiyaan's fleet has turned to piracy and revenge. The last thing he expects to find on a derelict passenger ship is an alluring human woman carrying contraband technology. And he definitely never expected her to worm her way into his heart...

Tap the cover to get your copy now or keep reading for a sneak peek. (Psst - Book one is free right now!)

Until next time!
Love, Tamsin

GLOSSARY

Ahen - an opiate-like drug.

Amai wood - a rich golden brown wood sought after for its buttery texture and sweet scent. The resin is used as an aphrodisiac on the planet Hy.

Ayabe - slightly astringent fermented leaves humans might think resembles cole slaw.

Bacca - a game that resembles frisbee golf.

Burendo - a Kirenai who excels at shapeshifting and is able to not only assume the form of other species, but coloration as well.

Fogarian - aliens with red hair and sideburns who live on a rocky, mountainous planet.

G'nax - a species that uses light to communicate attraction and arousal. They also have a symbiotic relationship with an eight-legged insectoid.

Hage - bald, wide-eyed alien that looks much like the iconic alien humans have circulated.

Happa trees - blue fronds resembling palms.

Hypawa - species with magma-colored eyes.

Ijin'en - four-legged herd animal raised for meat and well known for its stupidity.

Iki'i - empathic power.

Irn - a unit of measure. One planetary rotation around the Kirenai's sun.

Itoshi - beloved. Term of endearment.

Jiro - a unit of measurement equivalent to approximately two Earth hours.

K'ogai - the town near the palace on Kirenai Prime.

Kazhitu - nuts that look like sticky buns when baked. High in sugar, and tastes buttery and fruity.

Khargal - gray, horned aliens with stone-like skin and wings from the planet Duras ;)

Khensei - a toxin that causes Kirenai to denature into their resting state.

Kikajiru - my distracting one - a term of endearment.

Kirenai Prime - the Kirenai home planet. Purple and blue with swirling white clouds.

Klen - aliens who communicate via scent.

Kuro - a type of bitter, very black tea.

Kuzara - shit, damn, fuck.

Kryillian death swarm - tiny insectoid creatures that can kill a man within seconds by sucking his blood.

Matrix/cellular matrix - the term for a Kirenai's cellular mass.

Nezumi - a small downy animal with a stumpy tail and floppy ears found on most space stations.

Nilgawood - a tree used to make resin.

Oritsu - An expression of awe.

Popotan - the plant used to line ship interiors that provides oxygen, recycles water, is highly resistant to radiation, and can regenerate itself if damaged.

Qalqan - a species known for their healers. Good bedside manners due to their resistance to emotional fluctuation.

Resting state - a Kirenai's amorphous shape, like nakedness to humans, it is shown only to family or trusted friends.

Senburu - a galactic conglomeration of merchants who oppose the emperor's rule. Individual members are called *Senbur.*

Sireta Prime - a popular party planet.

Supo cloth - smart fabric for clothing that doesn't need buttons or zippers.

Teozhisa - a cart to carry people.

Tolonovone - a device that creates lighted markings on the skin. Used by G'naxians as part of their mating rituals.

Ukimi ice - beloved dessert with cool, spicy flavor like sweet mint.

Vatosangans - species with alabaster skin and blue or green hair who tend to be stocky or rounded. Planet is called Vatosang.

Zhinku weed - common in the popotan fields.

KIRENAI FACT SHEET

Kirenai are an all-male species of shapeshifters with a natural form (resting state) like an amoeba who usually assume a bipedal shape to interact with other species. Until the discovery of humans, Kirenai required a permanent pair-bond with a female of another species to produce offspring. All Kirenai traits are dominant and located on the Y chromosome; male offspring are fully Kirenai, while female offspring are fully of the mother's species.

Birth rates have been historically low, and over the ages, the population has been dwindling. Human females proved to be exceptionally receptive to impregnation, and do not require formation of a pair-bond to conceive. This has made Earth a target for black market slave traders who deal in "breeders." The Emperor has been making attempts to protect the population.

Regardless of the shape a Kirenai is in, he will be recognized as Kirenai by his skin and hair color. The most common hue is blue, although colors can be anywhere from mint green to lavender. Rare individuals called *burendo* can effect coloration outside this range. Kirenai blood is clear or slightly milky unless infected, when it grows murky to almost solid white.

All Kirenai have empathic abilities called Iki'i which make them capable of reading emotion and desire, as well as identifying individuals within their own species regardless of shape. This is the only Kirenai trait sometimes passed on to female progeny. The ability also makes the species as a whole consummate lovers because they can take actions and form attributes their partner finds most appealing. Bonded mates assume a permanent form pleasing to their mates; rarely can they force themselves into an alternate shape after bonding.

The average Kirenai life-span is approximately eight hundred human years. When a pair-bond is formed, a Kirenai passes a small genetic marker to his mate that mitigates the aging process, giving the mate a lifespan to match his own.

"I recognize your ship, Captain Qaiyaan." The voice coming over the ship's comm deepened with menace. "You're interfering with a legal salvage operation."

The two ships rotating helplessly outside Qaiyaan's port screen told a different story than the human on the comm was telling; an eyeful of stars peeked through the blackened hole piercing the Syndicorp passenger ship's hull, while the second, unmarked vessel's short-range lasers glowed from recent use. "Seems you ought to be a bit more generous," Qaiyaan drawled. "What with needing our help and all. I'm gonna take first crack at the salvage, then we'll get you your part. You can have whatever we leave behind."

"I warn you, don't touch that ship!" blustered the voice on the other end.

Normally Qaiyaan'd wish the other pirate captain well and move on. Not today. His crew hadn't had a profitable job in half a Denaidan year. This opportunity was too good to pass up. Besides, anyone who blew a hole in an unarmed passenger transport—Syndicorp or otherwise—left a sour taste in Qaiyaan's mouth. "I could simply wait here. My first mate estimated in half a day we'll have two ships in need of salvage. This is an awful deep part of space to find yourselves without a spare flux modulator."

"You fucking son-of-a-rakwiji-whore bastard! I have powerful friends, and I can make sure you never find safe harbor in this sector again!"

Qaiyaan crossed his arms and glared at the comm. "I'm the *only* friend you have in the galaxy at this moment, so I suggest you be polite."

Noatak, Qaiyaan's first mate, grinned at him from the navigator's seat, the copper sheen of his skin reflecting the multi-colored light from the control panels. The small cockpit, designed for humans, was barely big enough for the two Denaidan males to breathe at the same time. "Want me to take us in for soft docking?"

Qaiyaan watched the human pirate ship complete another slow, helpless turn in the port monitor. "Take us in, but keep an eye out for anything suspicious. Could be a Syndicorp trap."

"Pretty elaborate for a setup." Noatak shook his head, the metal beads decorating his long hair and beard clicking softly.

"Chances of blowing both in-line flux modulators at once *and* not having a spare? Either he's stupid, or it's a setup."

"I say he's stupid." Noatak adjusted the controls to nose the *Hardship* toward the passenger wreckage.

Qaiyaan rose from the captain's chair. Shit happened, especially to ships running less-than-legal activities. He ought to know, having just forked out the proceeds from their latest heist to retrofit a new hull onto the *Hardship's* battle-damaged frame. The black market repairman'd all but asked Qaiyaan to bend over and spread his cheeks. Rotten, cheating bastard.

Turning to the door, he paused and looked over his shoulder at Noatak. "Just be careful. Even if it's not a trap, Syndicorp'll be looking for their missing ship, and I don't want to be caught with our dicks out."

After sealing the control room door, he slid down the ladder to the cargo bay, booted feet clanging against the catwalk grating as he landed. "Mekoryuk! Tovik! All hands on deck!"

Mekoryuk poked his clean-shaven face out of the med bay. He was the only crew member who chose not to wear the customary full beard the Denaida prided themselves on, citing a doctor's need for cleanliness or some such *anaq*. "What is it?"

"Salvage mission. Assume zero atmo. No time for suits. Syndicorp could be riding our ass any minute. Where's Tovik?"

"Where else?" Mek tilted his head toward the end of the hall.

Qaiyaan left the doctor and strode to where the hatch to the engine room stood open. As captain, he could appreciate the well-oiled hum of a ship's engines, but Tovik was a bit too much in love with moving parts. Squatting next to the hole, Qaiyaan yelled, "Tovik! On deck ready for void! And bring a spare in-line flux modulator! Now!"

Knowing his crewmen would comply without further prodding, he headed for the airlock. Through the portal, he watched Noatak guide the magnetic grappler into place. The captain of the human ship was probably apoplectic, watching his cash cow get raped by another ship. *Tough luck.* Qaiyaan'd be sure to leave the replacement flux modulator within reach, but not until the *Hardship* was ready to hightail it out of there.

The first mate finessed the grappler toward the other ship's open airlock, his voice crackling over the internal comm to the cargo bay. "You sure you don't want to take time to suit up?"

Mekoryuk arrived with a med-kit over his shoulder, and Qaiyaan shot him a grin as he answered. "No suits. These *qumli* need the practice."

Tovik pounded up, feet bare as usual, his scruffy beard and hair not quite the full mane of a mature Denaida male. Qaiyaan scowled at him, looking pointedly at his gleaming copper feet. The youngster said he had better control of his ionic abilities if his skin was bare, but one of these days he was going to lose a toe, or worse. At least the boy carried the spare flux modulator, as requested.

While Noatak secured the flexi-tube between the ships, Qaiyaan filled in the other crew members. "I'm not sure what we'll find over there, but it's not likely to be pretty. Grab everything not nailed down. We'll sort our inventories later."

Mek asked, "What about survivors?"

"There's no life signs aboard." Qaiyaan pointed to the modulator in Tovik's hands. "That'll stay with the human ship once we leave. Can you give it a slow push their direction? I don't want it to reach them until we're long gone."

"You bet, Captain!" the young man nodded, likely already calculating trajectory and speed at which to push the thing.

"Stand fast for void!" Noatak's voice echoed through the cargo bay.

Qaiyaan barely had time to summon his ionic shell before the doors cracked open. A blast of air swept past, rattling the flexi-tube as it sucked into the other ship and out the gaping hole in its hull. The Denaidan's ability to withstand vacuum had made them one of the most sought-after races for Syndicorp marine crews before the catastrophe had ended their world. Now…

Now they were just pirates.

Concentrating on keeping his feet on the deck, Qaiyaan tapped his temple to activate his cochlear implant. A vestige of his days as a trooper, it came in handy in zero atmo when they couldn't bother with suits and the attached comms.

The three crewmen pushed themselves along the flexi-tube into the darkness of the other ship. Tovik, ever prepared, pulled a floodlight from his belt and slapped it to the inner wall of the passenger ship. The illumination exposed a passenger cabin surprisingly gutted of anything passenger-related. No nav-grav seats for humanoids, no methane tanks for garan'uks, not even any acceleration webbing for yanipa-nimayu. Instead, cargo containers of all shapes and sizes floated freely within the cabin, some cracked open and spilling their contents in haloes around them.

What the hell is this ship? Qaiyaan wondered. He'd been expecting the gruesome sight of space-bloated passengers. Not that he minded this alternative. He reached out and grabbed a floating package of hypodermic needles. *Medical supplies?*

He exchanged a glance with Tovik, who shrugged. Whatever this stuff was didn't matter; he'd much rather deal with salable goods than corpses.

Qaiyaan pushed toward the nearest container until he could get a hand on it and shoved the man-sized box toward the flexi-tube, relying on inertia to carry it most of the way. One after another, he moved containers, working until sweat coated his skin beneath his ionic shielding. Even in zero-G, it took effort to hold himself steady and force the heavy boxes into motion. At least twenty minutes passed before he grew light-headed. Using the ionic shell was much like a diver holding his breath, and he knew they'd soon have to come up for air. A tinny voice in his implant did the job for him. "We have incoming on long-range, Captain. Can't yet tell if it's Syndicorp, but they'll be in range for ID in eight minutes."

Anaq. They'd come looking faster than he'd expected. He raised his arm and caught the other men's attention, circling two index fingers overhead to tell them to wrap it up. The men dropped what they were doing and moved toward the exit.

As soon as the door sealed, blessed oxygen began to fill the bay, but it would be a few minutes before there was enough pressure to breathe. Still light-headed, Qaiyaan began helping secure the containers against the floor's mag-locks. He estimated they'd emptied at least half the salvage and was feeling quite pleased as Noatak began accelerating away from the derelict ship.

"Captain?" Mek called from behind a stack of containers.

At that same moment, Noatak's voice crackled through the bay's comm. "Confirmed Syndicorp ship closing in fast. We need to burn, ASAP."

"We need five minutes," Qaiyaan said, assessing the remaining cargo.

"Captain!" Mekoryuk called again. "We have a problem."

"What?" Qaiyaan leaned around the corner. Tovik and the medic stood over a cargo box, staring down at a portal in its surface. Blinking red light bounced off both their faces.

Tovik rubbed his hand vigorously across the small window. "Is that a girl?"

"You've got to be fucking kidding me." Qaiyaan slapped a mag clamp against the container he was securing and stood. "A cryo-pod? Who the hell picked that up?"

"You said grab everything," Tovik said. He looked up to meet Qaiyaan's gaze. "Can we keep her?"

Noatak came over the com again. "Captain, they're hailing us."

Qaiyaan scowled and thrust a finger at the cryo-pod. "She's not a *netorpuk* puppy, Tovik. Just secure the damn thing so we can burn. We'll figure out what to do with it later."

"That's the problem," Mek said. "The cryo's failing. She won't survive a burn in this state."

"Fuuuck." Qaiyaan stomped over to the pod. He should have known things were going too easy. Looking at the face through the glass, his mouth grew suddenly dry. A young woman with long charcoal hair lay inside, a crescent of dark lashes against her high cheekbones. The blinking red light near her head illuminated her perfectly sculpted features as if coating them with blood.

"Just vent it," Noatak spoke over the line. "Let Syndicorp pick it up."

Tovik grabbed the end as if claiming the pod as his own. "You can't do that. What if they miss her?"

Noatak answered, "Not our problem."

"You should see what she looks like..." Tovik continued.

Now wasn't the time to argue over crew shares of the spoils, but Qaiyaan felt a sudden desire to wrestle the pod away from his engineer and claim the contents for himself. He tamped down the feeling. If they didn't get moving immediately, Syndicorp troopers would shoot first and ask questions later.

Noatak's voice boomed over his thoughts. "*Anaq*! They just obliterated the human ship!"

Syndicorp is out for blood today. Clenching his jaw, Qaiyaan shoved Tovik aside and began pushing the box toward the airlock, averting his gaze from the breath-taking face inside. "If we vent her, they'll have to stop and pick her up, which'll give us more time to get away."

"But, Captain—" Tovik started.

"We're not murderers!" Mek shouted, moving to intercept the box.

The comm filled the bay again. "Captain, you're not going to like this." Noatak's voice had gone from excited panic to deadly quiet. Qaiyaan ceased pushing, turning to face the speaker as if he could read his first mate's face from here. Noatak only used that voice when something deadly was going on. "They took out the passenger ship, too. There's nothing left of either vessel but a haze of space dust."

The breath left Qaiyaan's body. Syndicorp'd destroyed their own ship? Why would they do that?

Mek moved close to the captain, his voice low. "Venting her is a death sentence."

Qaiyaan squeezed his eyes shut. Why could nothing ever be easy? This woman was probably some scrawny human female on an exorbitant corporate cryo-vacation or some such nonsense. But he couldn't just leave her, not to the mercy of space, and definitely not to a ship that was blowing up everything in its path. "How long do you need to wake her?"

"The waking cycle takes twenty minutes."

He leveled a glare at the medic. "I didn't ask how long it takes. I asked how long you need."

Mek shook his head. "I can pull her out now, but she'll take days to recuperate. And she'll still be too weak to strap in for burn."

"Days to recuperate is better than minutes to end up as space dust. Pull her. We can link our ionic shells to protect her during burn."

Mek's right eye twitched. "We're exhausted from scavenging in zero atmo. I'm not sure we can withstand the strain."

"Do you have a better suggestion? If you do, make it now, because we're out of time."

"They'll be in range in thirty seconds, Captain," Noatak clipped out, his voice still deadly steady.

Mek's jaw bulged, but he nodded. "Fine. I think I've got enough stims to keep us up and running afterward. But let's not make a habit of it."

Popping the pod's seals, Qaiyaan knelt to lift the frigid human from the padded interior. She was naked, her nipples peaked from the cold. His hand slid beneath her nicely rounded bottom, every ionic sensor in his skin aware of the contact. He tried to remain focused on her face instead of the silky smooth curve of her hip cradled against his chest. Her eyes fluttered but didn't open.

Laying her on the deck, he stretched out beside her, grounding himself to the metal decking. Enveloping her in his power. Locking his body against hers.

Tovik sat cross-legged at her head, his bare feet tucked beneath him, and placed both his hands on her shoulders. But his gaze was on her upright nipples. Come to think of it, Qaiyaan's were, too, so he couldn't blame the young engineer. Mek spread out along her other side. An unfamiliar twinge made Qaiyaan want to shove them both away.

Hoping he hadn't just given all four of them a death sentence, Qaiyaan called out, "Engage full burn."

Get your free ebook copy from your favorite bookstore > Rescued by Qaiyaan

INTERGALACTIC DATING AGENCY

Looking for more out of this world romance? Your local Intergalactic Dating Agency can help! These strong, smart, sexy aliens are on the prowl for mates, and humans like you are exactly what they're after. Jump in with Book 1 of any standalone trilogy from our crew of rock star SFR authors and make steamy first contact! Warning: abductions may or may not be included!

Grab more hunky alien action here:

http://romancingthealien.com

Untamed Instinct

Bewitched Shifter

Midnight Heat

Wild Child

<u>Kirenai Fated Mates (Intergalactic Dating Agency)</u>

Arazhi

Zhiruto

Iroth

****POST-APOCALYPTIC SCIENCE FICTION WRITTEN AS TAM LINSEY****

Botanicaust

The Reaping Room

Doomseeds

Amarantox

ABOUT THE AUTHOR

Once upon a time I thought I wanted to be a biomedical engineer, but experimenting on lab rats doesn't always lead to happy endings. Now I blend my nerdy infatuation of science with character-driven romance and guaranteed happily-ever-afters. My monsters always find their mates, with feisty heroines, tortured heroes, and all the steamy trouble they can handle. I promise my stories will never leave you hanging (although you may still crave more!)

When I'm not writing, I'll be in the garden or the kitchen, exploring Alaska with my husband, or preparing for the zombie apocalypse. I also love wine and hard apple cider, my noisy chickens, and attempting to crochet.

Interested in more about me? Join my VIP Club and get free books, notices, and other cool stuff!

www.tamsinley.com